The Biker's Wench

Jamie DeBree

Thank you for your purchase. For a free digital
copy of *The Biker's Wench*, please visit
BrazenSnakeBooks.com.

The Biker's Wench
ISBN 9780983198888
The Biker's Wench Copyright © 2011 Jamie M DeBree
Published by Brazen Snake Books
All rights reserved.

Edited by Carol R. Ward
Cover art by Heidi Sutherlin

For my husband.

Also by the Author

Tempest

Desert Heat

Chapter One

Monica gritted her teeth as someone started playing Buffalo Gals for the fifth time on the off-key piano in the corner. She stood with her back to the grand old mahogany bar, elbows propped up on either side and long, full skirts hiding the heel she hooked over the gold railing near the floor. Her feet were killing her, and she wondered for the millionth time how women in the 1800's had managed to wear the tall leather boots day in and day out. Maybe they'd be more comfortable after a few weeks of wear. She wondered if she'd be able to stay long enough to find out.

The saloon was busy, dusty wooden boards creaking as several guests exaggerated a two-step across the floor. Two of the other saloon girls were flirting with a small bachelor party in the corner, their childlike giggles ringing out over the occasional jingle of a spur. They played their parts well, laughing and sitting on the gentlemen's laps with breasts threatening to spill over tight corsets. Monica fought the urge to glance down at her own chest, slightly more covered by the chemise she'd pulled up underneath the laces of her own corset. Mavis, her boss and bartender had grinned when she saw it, but warned Monica that she needed to show more skin tomorrow night. Purely for the guests, she'd explained. While a slightly more modest costume may be more authentic, people didn't come to the Fantasy Ranch for history, they came for the fantasy. And this particular fantasy required the saloon girls to be slutty flirts. She wondered if there was a spot open on the race track. At least those girls got to wear jumpsuits, even if they didn't zip up all the way.

"Wench! Bring me a beer!" Monica stifled a groan. She was pretty sure that *wench* was a European term, but why would anyone here know that? She pushed away from the bar, glancing in the direction the command had come from.

Oh no.

Braden Thomas, the man her father insisted she had to marry, was leaning back in a chair sporting a cheap brown leather vest and a cheesy straw hat. He was staring right at her, a smug look on his cover model face. Looks could be so deceiving.

"Here you go, dear." Mavis pushed a round tray full of heavy glass mugs across the bar. "Don't keep 'em waiting now, you know how the menfolk get when they get thirsty." She winked and Monica took the tray, forcing her feet to carry her forward. How had he found her so quickly? She'd been so careful, using only cash, no cell-phone and she'd even ditched her car in Reno and gotten a ride out to the ranch. How did he keep finding her?

She set the mugs down one by one in front of Braden and his two friends. "Is there anything else I can get you, cowboys?" Braden returned the front legs of his chair to the floor with a thud.

"You know there is, darlin' - how much is horse-flesh like you going for these days?" His buddies laughed while he just sat back and grinned, but she saw the anger in his eyes. His patience was wearing thin, and she knew it was a dangerous game she was playing. She needed to leave. Now.

She edged away from the table, holding the empty tray in front of her like a shield. "Let me just ask the bartender, and I'll get back to you on that." Striding quickly to the bar, she handed the tray across and motioned for Mavis to lean in. "Do you think I could take just a quick five minute break? I really need to get some air - I'm feeling kind of faint."

The older woman frowned. "You a smoker? Because I can't have the customers seeing one of my girls smoking. It just wasn't done by women back then."

Yeah, right. She tried to look chastised. "I know it's a nasty habit, but I really need one - I could sneak out the back, go over behind the Double D?" No one would blink an eye at someone smoking outside of the biker bar next door. White vapors rolled out in waves whenever the front door opened or someone got tossed out the front window. It was surprising how often that happened.

"Fine, but cover up so no one knows you're from the saloon. And be back in exactly five minutes. We got customers to take care of."

The woman went back to wiping the wood down with a white rag, and Monica tried to walk normally through the swinging wooden doors in back and through the staff area. There was no doubt that Braden would come after her, it was just a question of when. As soon as she knew she was out of view from the main guest area, she ran out the back door and down the stairs, glancing quickly between the buildings as she raced behind the Double D.

And straight into a warm, leather-clad wall.

The impact nearly sent her flying backwards, her momentum stopped only by two steely hands grasping her upper arms. Thick fingers dug into her biceps and she cried out, instinctively struggling to get away. How had Braden gotten ahead of her? Panicked, she lashed out with her feet, kicking at his calves until he pulled her up tight against his chest, locking his arms around her.

"Dammit, woman. I'm not going to hurt you. Stop fighting."

It took a moment for the fact to sink in that the low, gravely voice did not belong to her ex-fiancé any more than the muscular physique. She stilled against the steady heartbeat at her ear and slowly tilted her face up to look at her captor. His face in shadow, she could just make out the harsh, angular lines of a strong chin and high cheekbones. A bandana covered his head, and a barely healed cut angled down beside his left eye. He was ruggedly handsome in a bad-boy sort of way, she decided as he finally lowered his arms and allowed her to step back. She shivered, the chilled night air reminding her that she'd forgotten to bring a coat. Not that it mattered. She'd have to leave now, so getting fired was the least of her concerns.

"Where's the fire?" He reached into his jacket and took out a pack of cigarettes, placing one between his lips. She waited for him to produce a lighter, but he put the pack away and then reached up to twist the filter end until an orange glow appeared at the tip.

She frowned. "What kind of a cigarette is that?"

He took it out of his mouth, blowing a thin stream of smoke into the air before he held the small stick out to her. "The kind that doesn't make other people sick. Theoretically speaking." Turning the hard plastic piece over in her fingers, she sniffed at first one end, then the other, and twisted the end. The light went out, and she handed it back to him.

"So where does the smoke come from?" In spite of herself, she leaned forward as he turned it back on and placed it between his lips. His cheeks hollowed as he inhaled, then lowered the cigarette and blew out a long stream of smoke into the air over her head.

"It's water vapor. We tried running the bar without smokes, but the customers complained that it wasn't realistic. So the boss found these so we could smoke 'em inside." He surveyed her, his gaze moving slowly down and back up her body as if she were a piece of art. "You work in the saloon. Where were you headed just now?"

Damn. She'd forgotten about Braden for a moment. He'd be coming any minute. "Um...I need to go to the dorm." Edging to the side, she snuck a peek down the alley, turning back to find him blocking her path. "I just need to get something..." Like clothes, so she could bum a ride back to Reno with one of the guests. It was past time to go. She moved to step around him, and he moved in front of her again.

"Shifts aren't over until ten." The casual comment had an authoritative edge to it that gave her pause, even as she looked down the alley again. There was no mistaking the tall, lanky shadow coming towards them, and her heart raced as time ran out.

Glancing back at the biker, she kept her voice low. "Please - I don't know who you are, but I really have to get out of here. There's a man looking for me...well, he found me here, and I really need to go. Right now. I --"

"There you are, Monica." Braden stepped out of

the alley and reached for her arm. "Let's just stop all this nonsense and go home now, shall we? You're father is very worried, and we've got a wedding to plan."

She backed away, her shoulder pressing into the corner of the saloon. "I'm not going anywhere with you. And my father can just go to hell. Leave me alone!" She pivoted on the edge of the building and turned to run, catching a heel in the hem of her dress. Hitting the ground hard, she rolled a few times, then pushed up on her elbows and got to her feet just as Braden grabbed her arm. She pulled, but couldn't twist out of his iron grasp.

Behind her, someone wrapped an arm around her waist and pulled her backwards. "Get your hands off my woman."

Confusion, fear and anger all flickered across Braden's face as he let go, taking a step back. "Who the hell are you?"

The biker casually flung an arm around her shoulders. "Harley Majors - I own this place. I'd ask who you are, but frankly, I don't care. You're leaving."

"That's my fiancée you're wrapped around friend, so just hand her over and we'll get out of your hair."

Harley glanced down at the woman tucked securely under his arm - Monica, the man had called her. This close he could see the weary lines on her face and the haunted, fearful look in her chocolate-brown eyes. He wondered how long she'd been running from this guy and more importantly, what kind of trouble he was getting himself into by helping her out. The last three women he'd gotten close to had done their best to ruin his name and take him for everything he was worth. Stepping in this time had been instinctive, and it was probably going to bite him in the ass.

Then she pressed closer against him, sliding a hand around his waist, and he knew what he had to do. "You're not my friend, sir - and she's not your fiancée either. It's time you moved on. She's with me now, and you're not welcome back. Hit the road, or I'll have you escorted off my property." He moved in front of Monica, hoping Tony and Elvis would come looking for him soon. His lawyers had warned him against hitting anyone else after the last one nearly got the ranch in the law suit. It would have helped if the guy's wife hadn't lied about her role in the affair.

"You don't know who you're messing with, Mr. Majors." The man shook a finger in Harley's face, a gesture that once would have earned him a broken digit. "You just made the worst mistake of your life. And you." He peered around Harley's shoulder where Monica was standing. "This isn't over. It's never going to be over until you come home and do what's right."

"Go to hell, Braden."

Harley hid a smile at her command, relieved to see his two bouncers striding down the alley towards them. "I believe these two will be happy to escort you," he said, pointing over Braden's shoulder.

Braden glanced at Monica one last time then stalked off, pushing between the two bouncers who followed him out. Harley watched until they got to the main road. Clearly the woman needed help, and a radical idea that just might benefit both of them whispered through his head. He'd been considering it for awhile now, but hadn't been happy with the choices available. With this woman though, it just might work.

He swore under his breath when he turned to find the area deserted. He pulled his cell phone out of his jacket, shaking his head as he started walking towards the staff quarters. Out here, it made sense to have the staff stay on site all the time, so room and board was provided.

"Cindy? Harley. I need a new employee's room number - I don't know her last name, but her first name is Monica." He waited while she looked up the record, then disconnected and called the bar to let them know he wouldn't be back tonight. The more he thought about it, the more he was sure his idea would work. As long as she would agree not to fall in love with him, that is.

He found room number 502, and hesitated only a moment before rapping three times on the metal door.

* * *

Monica froze when someone rapped on her door.

She'd seen the two big men go after Braden - had he somehow slipped past them and back into the ranch? He wouldn't know her room number though. That meant it had to either be Mavis from the saloon or that biker - Harley. A thrill ran under her skin as she remembered his warm, solid touch and that earthy, all male scent that had enveloped her as he pulled her close. Now that was a man a girl could fall hard for, if she was looking.

Which she wasn't, of course.

She tossed the last few items of clothing into her bag, trying to ignore the fact that he was probably standing outside her door at that moment, looking all rough-and-tumble sexy in biker gear. It probably wasn't the real him anyway. That was the whole point of Fantasy Ranch. She wondered what he was like when he wasn't working. He'd said he was the owner, and an image of him in a suit and tie popped into her head as she zipped her bag closed. No doubt about it, she thought, grinning. That man would look hot no matter what he was wearing. It had clearly been too long since she'd gotten laid.

"Monica - it's Harley. I know you're in there, I can hear you moving around. Open the door. I've got a proposition for you."

She paused, her hand on the doorknob. It didn't matter what he had in mind. Now that Braden had found her it was only a matter of time before her father knew where she was, and either sent reinforcements or came to get her himself. She had to leave, tonight if possible, and get as far away as she could before morning. The one thing she didn't have was transportation, and maybe if she explained Harley could arrange for her to get a lift into town. Bad as it was having to ask, she hadn't been around long enough to make any friends, and he seemed to be in a helpful mood. She took a breath, let it out slowly, and steeled herself against the desire already building deep within as she opened the door.

There was no way to prepare for how the sight of him under the fluorescent hall lights did funny things to her stomach. This time she could see the way his jeans fit like a second skin, the planes of his muscles under the tight black t-shirt that peeked out from his worn leather jacket, and the piercing blue eyes that pinned her in place under his stare. She'd been wrong. No way in hell would this man ever wear a suit.

"Can I come in?" That low, raw voice sent shivers up her spin as she stepped back, gesturing for him to enter. She tried to remember what it was she wanted to say, but her mind was curiously blank. Her body was humming though, a low throb of need that radiated out from her core and made her want to tear off her clothes and offer him anything he wanted.

Instead she sat in a chair across from where he'd settled on the couch, and mentally chastised herself for not staying focused. "Thanks for helping me out back there - I appreciate it. But I really do have to get going," she said, thankful that her voice sounded mostly normal. "Braden, the man you kicked out - he'll be back for me, probably with my father's men. They're mad because I won't play their little business merger game, and I'm sorry I got you involved. If you could just have someone give me a ride--"

Harley held up one hand. "Whoa there, slow down. It's Monica, right?"

"Monica Burns," she replied, dropping her gaze to stare at his black leather boots. "Though I suppose I'll have to change that too. It's the only thing I haven't left behind yet."

"Your choice," he said, bringing her attention back to his face. She could see him thinking, assessing as he looked at her, it was an unsettling feeling. "But if we're gonna get hitched, might be more convincing if we have the same last name."

Chapter Two

The silence stretched thick between them as the clock on the wall faithfully ticked off the seconds. Monica tried to comprehend what he'd just said, but she couldn't have heard him correctly. He did not just tell her they were getting married. He didn't look stupid. She narrowed her eyes, searching his face for any sign of mirth and finding none.

It was way past time for her to go. She swallowed hard. "I think I heard you wrong. I'm sure I did. But I really do have to go, so if you could just..." she stood, picking her duffel up off the floor and tossing it over her shoulder as she turned to reach for the door. But instead of cool metal, her fingers closed around hot, leathery skin, and she jumped back as if burned. "What the hell?"

Harley was standing in front of the door, blocking her path. "Just hear me out," he said, crossing his arms over that broad chest. His spicy-sweet scent was hypnotizing at this range and she stepped back, trying to regain some semblance of free thought that didn't involve jumping his bones. Why was he so irresistible? She dropped down to sit on the bed, trying to decide if maybe it wasn't worth a quick roll in the covers to get him out of her system before she moved on. Glancing up, she noticed those incredible lips were moving again, and tried to tune in.

"--so I figure if we get married, those women will stop trying to sue me for everything I'm worth, and your dad and his pansy-ass hotshot there won't be able to do anything to you. We stay married for a year, then part amicably."

He paused, uncrossing his arms to push his thumbs into the front pocket of his jeans, leaving his fingers to frame the prominent bulge in front. Well-endowed might be an understatement in this case. Monica tore her gaze away, forcing herself to look back up as the heat rose in her cheeks. Surely he hadn't missed the direction her thoughts were wandering. Most men would be flattered.

The cool, focused look in his eyes said he wasn't most men. His words washed over her like ice water, anger building as the full intent of his statement hit home.

"So if I've got this straight, you think that since my father wants to force me to marry his guy, I'll jump at the chance to get them both off my back by marrying some guy I just met instead." She shook her head, curling her hands into the bedspread to keep them from forming fists. "I'm not stupid, and I don't want to marry anyone. What's in it for you?" He opened his mouth, but she held up one finger. "Aside from side stepping annoying palimony suits from your groupies, I mean. Maybe you should just try keeping it in your pants for awhile. Easier than marrying me, and women are less likely to sue if you're not screwing them over."

Her pulse raced as he pushed off the wall and stalked over to stand in front of her. Perhaps that last comment hadn't been such a good idea. Unfortunately now his waist - and everything just below - was right at eye level. She licked her lips and scooted farther back on the bed to look up at him, her stomach fluttering. He braced a hand on either side of her, his face stopping just inches from hers as his heat surrounded her. He glanced at her mouth and for a moment she thought those gorgeous full lips would settle over hers. Then his eyes were on hers again and she nearly gasped at the anger and frustration they held.

"I plan to do just that. Which is exactly why this marriage will work for both of us, and why you need to stop looking at me like that." He pushed back, standing to pace in front of the bed as she willed her heart to slow down. Leave it to a guy to make no sense at all.

She shook her head. "I'm confused - how is getting

married going to help you not get laid? Unless..." She paused, his meaning becoming clear. "Oh. You want a marriage but no sex." She considered that for a moment while he sank down into the chair by the door. She frowned. "Why would you do that? Are you gay?"

"No." He rubbed his neck with one hand, his gaze on the floor. "Some news rag got a hold of my financial statements last year and published them in an article calling me the most eligible rich guy in the area - all bullshit. But now because of that article, women throw themselves at me all the time trying to get my money. The last one's husband actually told her to seduce me and then claimed I forced her. My life's been hell since that article and the lawyers say it will help if I get married." He exhaled a long, slow, resigned breath. "All I need from you is just to pretend like you're madly in love with me so other women know I'm off limits." He looked up, tilting his head thoughtfully. "I'll pay you. I'll still help you get your old man and that other dude off your back, but I'll pay you to be legally married to me for one year. My secretary says she might as well be my wife, and she gets forty thousand a year - is that enough?"

Monica's eyes grew wide at the sum. "You want to pay me forty thousand dollars. For a marriage with no sex. And you'll help me deal with my family issues." She rubbed her face with her hands and sighed, a sound of disbelief and resignation. Harley sat forward, resting his elbows on his knees. He was confused at her hesitation. She had a big problem, and he could solve it. He'd never understand why women made everything so complicated.

"Just think of it as a promotion," he said, grinning as he looked pointedly at the costume she still wore. "You're already an employee here. Instead of being a saloon girl, you can consider yourself my personal wench for the next year."

He watched as her face turned bright red. She stood and slung her bag over her slender shoulder with so much force it nearly spun her around. "I am no one's wench," she said, her voice shaking. "And the whole point of my being here was to avoid getting married, so the fact that you would even ask..." She stomped over to the door and twisted the knob, nearly bashing his head with her bag as she flung the door open. "You men are all alike, you know that? A woman should have a choice in these things, and I'll be damned if I'm going to marry you or anyone else. And you can take your money and burn it for all I care. I'm outta here." She stepped into the hall and slammed the door shut behind her. Harley winced.

"That could have gone better," he mused as he got to his feet. He made sure the lock still worked, then secured the door behind him as he jogged down the hall. It probably wasn't a good idea to follow her, but something told him this wasn't over yet. At the very least she still needed a ride into town. Maybe a little wind in her hair would calm her down. *Not that she*

isn't stunning when she's all riled up. He spotted her walking under a street light half way to the front gate.
Those big brown eyes flashed fire when she was mad,
and her skin flushed such a pretty pink hue. He
wondered if she'd look that way underneath him in
bed, not that he would ever find out.

He stopped long enough to make sure there was a
spare helmet on his bike, and straddled the big machine, firing up the engine with a roar. Unless he had
completely misread Monica Burns, she wouldn't be
able to resist a ride on nearly eight hundred pounds of
chrome and steel. The woman was all fire and heat,
and his crotch tightened at the thought of her taking
him out for a ride. Probably just as well she'd turned
him down. He wasn't at all sure he'd be able to keep
his hands off her if they were together night and day.

He pulled up ahead of her as she walked, shutting
the bike down so she could hear him. "At least let me
give you a ride into town." He held out the spare helmet, watching the emotions play across her face as
she considered his offer. She was still upset, but he
saw her take in the lines of the bike, her eyes following the ice blue flames along the side, the shiny
chrome fenders, and finally back up over the black
leather seat. His cock twitched at her open admira-
tion. There wasn't anything as sexy as a chick ogling
his bike. Unless she was ogling him, of course, like
she had back in her room. It had been all he could do
to keep from taking her right then and there. "Come

on, Monica. I won't bite." He winked, pleased at the
way her breath hitched a little at his words. She
moved forward, slowly to take the helmet.

"What about my bag?" Her voice was husky and
seductive; though he was sure she hadn't intended it
to be. Ignoring the instinct to toss her over his
shoulder and carry her back to his place, he took the
bag from her and strapped it onto the carry rack, then
swung his leg over again. She pulled the helmet over
her head, struggling a little to get it situated, then
walked over to swing up behind him.

"Ever ridden before?" he asked, feeling her hands
just barely touch his sides. She held herself rigid as he
kicked up the stand, and he anticipated how it would
feel when she was pressed fully against him.

"No."

He chuckled, reaching back to pull her arms tighter
around him. He could feel her trembling as she
settled tighter against him, still stiff as a board. "Hang
on, honey. You're gonna love this." He turned the key
and she automatically locked her arms fully around
him, her breasts pressing into his back and her legs
snug around him. God she felt good. He drove out
onto the highway and opened up the throttle, speeding down the open road. It wasn't long before she
melted against him, her body moving in perfect time
with his as they turned a wide corner and crested a
small hill. The lights of Reno twinkled brightly in the
distance, and he eased back on the throttle as they

passed a cop car sitting in the barrow pit. A quarter mile down the road, red and blue lights were flashing behind them.

* * *

Monica reluctantly loosened her grip as Harley pushed his helmet off, peeling her body away from his back, trying to ignore the keen sense of loss that followed. She'd never dreamed that riding a motorcycle could be so exhilarating, so...sensual. Even now her core was still fitted tightly to his backside, her thighs wrapped tightly around his, and when she moved to slide back, his hand locked down on her leg, firmly but gently holding her in place.

"Just sit tight. This shouldn't take long." His grip turned to a caress, sending tingling electrical pulses up her leg to her hips as a uniformed officer approached from the side.

"Evening, Harley. Nice night for a ride."

Harley gave a curt nod. "Sure is. Something wrong, Kurt? I'm pretty sure I wasn't speeding."

"No, no you weren't." He shined his flashlight up to peer at Monica's helmet. She turned away from the brightness. "Ma'am, I'll need to you to take that off, please."

She struggled to get free, finally finding the right angle to pull the molded headgear off. Holding it awkwardly under one arm, she brushed her tangled hair out of her face, holding up a hand to shield her eyes from the light.

"That's her!"

She whipped her head around at Braden's voice, instinctively holding tighter to Harley as she watched her nemesis run over from the police car. He stopped by the officer, panting at the effort of running ten whole feet. What had Harley called him? Pansy-ass. Right. She worked to keep a smile off her face as a warm hand squeezed her thigh.

"This guy says you kidnapped his fiancée," Kurt said, tilting his head at Harley. "I thought you were gonna stay away from the ladies for awhile after that last rape charge."

Between her legs, Monica could feel his hips and legs stiffen up. "Jury found me innocent, you know that. Monica's with me of her own free will, isn't that right?"

"Yes." She swallowed, fear coursing under her skin. She'd never meant for anyone to get hurt, and now this man was being forced back into a nightmare because of her. She had to make sure he didn't pay for her decisions. "Braden's been stalking me. He's the one you should be questioning. He followed me all the way from Chicago."

The officer glanced at Braden, then back to Monica. "That doesn't explain why your father filed a missing persons report two months ago. He's been looking for you for awhile now. Most people don't just run off like that unless something's wrong."

"I--" Monica started to tell the story, then re-membered the last time she'd told the authorities any-thing. Her father had retaliated by insisting she wasn't in her right mind and that she needed psychiatric help. It had taken a lot of talking and a midnight bus ticket to get out of that mess. Harley's fingers rubbed her leg, returning her to the present.

"She came out to meet me," he said, deliberately reaching back to lace his fingers with hers. The con-tact was soothing, and she hung on, listening to his mellow voice as he continued. "We met over the in-ternet, and fell in love. I asked her to marry me to-night." He glanced back over his shoulder, his warm eyes locking with hers in a silent plea. "Tell them your answer, honey."

She hesitated. He was giving her a choice. Either take his deal, or take her chances with the police. As far as she could tell, there wasn't really a third option available, and she started trembling, knowing she was trapped either way. He squeezed her hand tight and released it, along with his gaze as he faced Kurt again. He took a breath, as if he were about to speak.

"Yes," she blurted out, her voice ringing louder than she'd intended. "I mean, yes, we're getting mar-ried." Heat suffused through her as Harley's hand caressed her thigh, and she was sure her face was beet red. Braden kicked a rock hard, sending it flying out into the desert.

"I don't believe it. You're lying," he yelled, pointing his finger at Harley. "You put her up to this, you bastard. Arrest him, officer. She belongs to me."

"I don't belong to anyone," Monica said, irked at the implication. "I'm marrying Harley because we're in love. That's all you need to know." She flinched as Harley reached down and grabbed one foot, pulling it up over his lap. He twisted and grasped her waist, then swung her around before she could protest so she was straddling his legs, tight against his arousal. He guided her arms up around his neck, and she hung on, if for no other reason than she felt like she'd fall over backwards at any second.

He stared into her eyes, his lips curved into a wicked grin. "She belongs *with* me," he growled, the sexy timbre sending a flood of moisture between her legs as he covered her mouth in a searing kiss.

Chapter Three

Monica couldn't think, much less breathe. Her senses were overwhelmed as Harley plundered her mouth with his tongue, stroking her higher and higher with every thrust against her lips. She rocked her hips against the hard ridge in his jeans, pressed her chest against his and nearly whimpered in disappointment when he pulled back after one last nibble at her bottom lip.

She prepared herself for the worst before she opened her eyes. Had she really just agreed not to have sex with this man for an entire year? Looking up into his intense blue gaze, she hoped like hell he wasn't serious. Because there was no way could she live with him and be expected to keep her hands off such a tasty treat.

"I think we get the point." The sheriff's amused voice broke the spell, reminding her that they had an

audience. Heat fused with excitement at the thought
of the display she'd just been part of, quickly followed
by embarrassment as the sheriff's lips turned up.
"Why don't you two take this show back to the ranch,
and I'll escort Mr. Thomas here back to the hotel. I
think we've seen what we needed."

Braden stepped forward, hands balled into fists at
his side. "You bitch. You haven't heard the last of
me." Monica leaned into Harley, her hands gripping
his ribcage as he pulled her to his chest, turning a
shoulder towards Braden in a clearly possessive move.

"Come on, Mr. Thomas." The sheriff took
Braden's arm and pulled the man aside, following
when he pulled away until they got back to the cruis-
er. The flashing lights went out a couple seconds after
they got in the car, and Monica watched them drive
away over the black leather-wrapped bicep of
her...*fiancé*. She leaned back slowly, shivering as the
cool night air took the place of his warmth. She
wanted to snuggle into him again and pretend that
they were really a couple. That he wasn't just another
man who wanted to use her for his own gain. At least
Harley only seemed interested in a short-term lease.
Best deal she'd been offered yet, even if the terms
were less than desirable. Though maybe he'd renego-
tiate, considering the electricity between them.

Finally gathering the courage to look up, she saw
him staring out across the desert, toward the lights of
Reno. Denying the urge to reach up and trail kisses

over the hard line of his angular jaw, she lost her balance as she tried to shift back on the seat. The motion pushed her harder into Harley's groin and he twitched between her legs. Those intense blue eyes met hers for a long moment as he grasped her waist, lifting her easily off his lap so she could swing her leg across to stand beside the bike. It took all she had to keep her knees from buckling as he pulled away

"This isn't going to work." His voice was husky, and stared down at his bike as he spoke. "Put your helmet back on. I'll take you into town, and buy you a plane ticket. You'll at least get a head start before they come looking for you again." He pulled on his own helmet and started the engine, revving the engine loud enough to drown out any protest she might have made. Monica stood frozen for a moment, her head spinning at the unexpected words as she tried to decide whether he was insulting her or just crazy.

She didn't want to run anymore. He'd offered her a way out, and the thought that he could actually help her get her life back had taken root in her mind. Freedom was only a year away, and after offering her all that he was just going to dump her on the first flight out? Like hell. She crossed her arms over her chest and stared, willing him to shut down the bike so they could talk. He stroked the engine again, clearly impatient to get moving. *Screw that.*

Grabbing the helmet off the back of the bike, she marched around to stand in the headlight beam where he could see her clearly. Lifting it over her head, she slammed the heavy item into the dirt, crossed her arms over her chest and waited. Several long moments passed before he shut down the motor and yanked his own head gear off. He swung a leg over the machine and strode toward her, his expression hidden in the darkness until he was standing so close she nearly took a step back.

"What the hell is wrong with you?" He leaned in, his breath warm on her face. "I just offered to pay your way anywhere out of here you want to go, and you start throwing my stuff around?" He stared at her a few more seconds before stepping back, rubbing a hand over his neck as he turned away. "I should have just handed you over to the sheriff." He turned back and put his hands on his hips, casting a striking profile in the dim moonlight as he waited.

Monica shivered, fighting back tears that had been close to the surface since Braden had walked into the saloon earlier that night. "I don't want to leave," she said quietly, looking down at the dark dirt. "You said you could help me, and I promise to do whatever you want. I can help you too." Looking up, she walked slowly to stand in front of him, her fingers sliding up his chest. "I can't run anymore. I'm tired. I don't want live like this." He flinched under her touch, but didn't pull away, and she hooked her hands lightly around his neck. "I'll do anything you want," she said, placing a soft kiss at the base of his throat. "Anything." She nibbled her way up the side of his neck to lick that scar on his jaw that had intrigued her earlier and tugged on his neck, wanting to feel his mouth against hers again.

Iron fingers circled her wrists, and pried her hands away as he forced her back, holding her in front of him at arm's length. The tears she'd been holding back escaped, spilling over her cheeks and she closed her eyes, bowing her head in defeat as she twisted out of his grasp. Humiliation flooded through her at the thought of what she'd done. Was this what she'd been reduced to then - a woman willing to trade her body for protection? She might as well go back to her father, since she'd obviously lost sight of what she was running from in the first place.

Turning away, she swiped at her face with her half-frozen fingers. Not only had she become the very thing she'd always feared, but she'd offered herself up to a man who didn't want her. She might as well just crawl out into the desert and disappear.

"You don't understand," Harley said, frustration in his gravely voice. "I can't be around you, not after tonight. It's better for both of us if you just go."

She shrugged and walked over to the discarded helmet, shaking it off before stowing it under her arm. "I get it," she said, avoiding his gaze. "It's okay. I'm sorry I threw myself at you like some sort of...saloon girl." Smoothing over her skirt, she supposed she'd need to pay him back for the costume. "I'm just tired and it's been so..." She took in a deep breath, forcing a carefree smile to her lips. "Never mind. If you would just drop me off near a hotel where I could find a phone, I'll take it from there. You've already given me far more help than you'll ever know, and I appreciate it."

She walked past him to stand by the bike and pulled the helmet on over her head, keenly aware of him following barely two steps behind. "Where will you go?" he asked as she lifted one leg and awkwardly straddled the motorcycle.

"I don't know," she replied, her shoulders lifting slightly. "I never know until I get there - I just run until I find somewhere that seems safe. Somewhere my father might overlook, at least for awhile."

***

Harley stared at the woman on his bike, her slim body out of proportion to the large black head gear framing her face. The way she'd felt pressed against him on the ride out had been amazing, and when she'd been draped across his lap, her hot center pressed against his cock, he'd nearly come undone. Keeping her with him, even for the short jaunt into town was dangerous. Women threw themselves at him all the time, but he hadn't wanted one quite this badly in a long time.

Marrying her was a really bad idea, lawyers be

damned. The fact that he couldn't keep his hands off her had the potential to create exactly the sort of emotional attachment he wanted to avoid. Unfortunately, men like her father only understood one thing. *Possession.* Until Monica was married off to a man strong enough to claim ownership, she'd get no peace from her own private nightmare.

Staring into her stoic brown eyes, he exhaled long and slow. Helping her the first time had been a mistake. Kissing her had been an even bigger one. The whole thing had been his idea though, and even though he knew it would probably be the biggest mistake of his life, he also knew there was no way he could just send her off to be hunted down by her father and his lackey again. He'd offered protection, and she'd get it. He hoped to hell she didn't take him for all he was worth when all was said and done.

Resigned to his fate, he pulled on his own helmet and straddled the bike in front of her, reaching back to pull her hands forward when she didn't automatically hold on to his waist. Satisfied she was secure, he started the machine and made a careful U-turn before gunning the engine. Her fingers flexed into his ribs as he drove back toward the ranch. The temperature had dipped lower, and he could feel her shivering against his back as she gave in and snuggled close to his heat. When he finally pulled into the ranch, she was plastered so tightly against him he wondered if she'd ever come off. Strangely, the idea didn't frighten him like it should have.

"Monica?" He removed his headgear and glanced over his shoulder after he turned off the engine, but she didn't move. "Hey, Princess. We're home." He grasped her ice-cold hands and pried them from around his waist. Swinging a leg over and off the bike, he stood and gently lifted the helmet off her head. Her gaze was as icy as her fingers.

"What do you want from me?" She wrapped her arms tightly over her chest. "First you want to marry me, no sex. Then you kiss me and it's incredible and your response is to put me on the first plane out of town. Now we're back here and I'm confused and tired and I really need to disappear before my father's goons get here. They're a lot scarier than Braden, trust me. So stop jerking me around, dammit!" She turned away, head bowed and shoulders hunched as she scuffed the toe of her boot in the dirt.

He reached out to touch her shoulder, but she stepped away. "I suppose I deserve that," he said, moving to her side. "Come on. Let's get this settled."

He took her hand in his, tightening his grip when she tried to pull it back. Pulling her along behind him he pulled out his cell phone with the other hand and dialed his assistant as they walked down the alley behind the Double D. "Cindy, I need you to call Pete. Have him meet me at the chapel. Yes, we'll need witnesses."

Monica tried to take her hand back, and he looked

back, grinning at the fire in her eyes. It wasn't just anger, he was sure. He stopped abruptly, yanking her off
balance so he could wind his arm around her back her
as she fell against his chest. "Sure, come on down.
You may as well meet the new missus." He hung up
just in time to keep her from wiggling out of his
grasp.

"Let me go!"

He tightened his grip. "No," he said, using the
same tone of voice he'd developed as a bouncer to
calm and control. Her eyes widened as he bent down
to touch his lips once, twice, three times to hers.
Straightening, he looked into her eyes again, the
arousal and need mirrored there nearly his undoing.
"Let's go get married, so your immediate problem is
solved. I promise those guys won't lay one finger on
you. Then we'll figure out what's next, take one thing
at a time. Okay?"

She looked down at his chest, staring for a long
moment while she nibbled her lower lip. Finally she
nodded. "Fine."

"Atta girl." He released her and held out his hand,
pleased when she took it voluntarily. "Regardless of
the circumstances, I think you're going to like this.
Most women do."

He winked and led the way between the saloon and
several more buildings, each with its own specialty
theme. At the end of the alley, there was a small
chapel across the road, with a faux cemetery to one

side and a wide park with a white gazebo to the other, barely visible in the darkness. The chapel was white with a tall bell tower and the door stood open, a warm rose-colored light spilling out onto the stepping stone walkway.

He stopped at the wrought iron arch over the main gate, and looked down at her, finally remembering the costume she had on. The laces were tight across the center, and sometime during the night the shirt underneath her corset had slipped, allowing her cleavage more room than he remembered seeing when she'd come out of the saloon. Would she let him free her the rest of the way after the ceremony? How could he resist, if she offered?

She stared up at him, one eyebrow raised and her mouth turned up in a smirk. "Like what you see, Mr. Majors?"

"You have no idea." He grinned and crooked his arm, offering his elbow like the gentleman he wasn't. "Ready?"

"Ready." Monica slid her hand under his arm like the lady she wasn't, and forced her feet up the walk. *This is the biggest mistake of my life.*

She stepped over the threshold and nearly jumped out of her skin as a tall, long-legged blond in a very short maid's costume entered through a doorway to the right.

"A lady of the night - a good choice, brother dear." The woman's voice practically hummed with sex, bringing a blush to Monica's cheeks. A slight accent made her wonder how they'd managed to find a real live French woman to play the maid here. No doubt she was very well paid.

"Knock it off, Bets." Harlan's annoyed tone snapped Monica out of her musing. She looked and them both in turn, the woman's words sinking in. This was Harley's sister? "Monica, this is my sister Betsy. Betsy, would you show Monica to the dressing room, and let her pick out a gown? I need to find Ian."

"He's in the sanctuary," Betsy said, dropping the accent. Her lips curved up in a smile and she turned to Monica, her eyes glancing down and back up her frame. "You come with me - I know just the dress."

Too dazed to argue, Monica followed Betsy down the rose-colored hall to a small door on the right. She was ushered inside, finding herself surrounded by tall racks of what appeared to be five different styles of wedding dresses in every size, plus racks of the same bridesmaid dress in a rainbow of colors beyond. The door closed behind her, and she turned as the lock snapped home to see Betsy leaning against the wall, staring thoughtfully. Finally, she spoke.

"I know you're not in love with him, so why are you marrying my brother?"

Monica sank down onto a large upholstered stool, exhaling long and slow. "He's trying to protect me," she said, realizing how weak that made her sound the second the words crossed her lips. "My father wants me to marry this other guy, and I ran away. But he's coming to get me and take me back. He won't give up easily. Your brother is strong and confident and my dad respects that. He might leave me alone if he thinks I'm married to Harley."

"So you're just going to use him until your dad leaves you alone and then leave? Why would Harlan agree to that?"

Monica wasn't sure just how much Harley would appreciate her telling his sister about his predicament, so she just shrugged. "I offered to leave. This was his idea. The deal is for one year."

Betsy tilted her head, her eyebrows raised. "Interesting." Pushing off the wall, she walked past and Monica stood, following her deeper into the rows of satin and tulle. When they reached the back of the room, she pulled open a closet door and stepped in to take a garment bag off the clothes rod, holding it out to Monica. "This is your dress. And it's not a loaner - it's yours to keep. I'll wait by the door while you change - holler if you need any help." Avoiding Monica's eyes, she brushed past and strode back toward the front of the room.

Monica frowned, hanging the bag on a nearby hook to the side of a large mirror. She pulled the zipper down slowly to reveal a simple strapless bone-colored sheath with an intricate vine pattern of seed pearls hand sewn around both the top and the knee-length hem. The style was timeless, classic and yet she had the feeling it was very old, a perfectly preserved antique. Stepping back, she shook her head. There must be some mistake. This was someone's heirloom, one of those dresses you pass down over generations. What was Betsy doing letting her wear it, much less telling her to keep it? She turned to find the other woman watching her, arms folded across her chest.

"I can't wear this," Monica said, waving a hand toward the garment. "Something tells me this is supposed to be yours."

Betsy nodded. "It was our mother's. She gave it to me to wear on my wedding day." She let out a long breath. "The thing is, I'm in love with a man who isn't going to marry me, ever. And I saw the way you and my brother looked at each other. I think mom would have wanted you to wear it, no matter why you're marrying him." She walked over to the dress, taking it carefully out of the bag. When she held it out draped over both arms, a long train that hadn't been visible before spilled out in a riot of creamy satin, displaying more of the beautiful beadwork Monica had been admiring. "Please. Harlan deserves that much for helping you, don't you think?"

Reluctantly, Monica took the dress, marveling at how smooth the fabric felt after all these years. To wear it would desecrate the memory of Harley's mother, that much she knew for sure. But was Betsy right? Would it make Harley happy to see her wearing it? Part of her said no. The other part pushed her to hurry up and make a decision. He was waiting, after all.

"Okay," she said finally, her voice barely over a whisper. She laid the dress over a chair and looked around, grateful Betsy had apparently gone. Quickly stripping out of the saloon girl outfit, she pulled the dress on and zipped it up the side, then turned to examine her profile in the big mirror. It fit perfectly, hugging her curves as if it had been made especially for her.

She tried to blink back tears of guilt and longing, wishing that for one moment, she could pretend that everything was real. But she couldn't. Instead of wearing a dress lovingly passed down by her mother, hers was meant for someone else. Rather than marrying a man she loved and couldn't imagine living one more day without, she was using marriage as a means to solve a problem. Everything was wrong. She brushed furiously at the tears on her face with one hand while reaching for the zipper with the other. So much was already wrong with her life. She wouldn't add this to her sins, and she certainly wouldn't drag Harley into it. There had to be somewhere she could hide until her father had gone...

Heavy footsteps came closer and somewhere in the back of her mind she registered that they were too firm and deep to be Betsy's stilettos. She wiped her face with both hands, blinking quickly in an attempt to compose herself as Harley came around the corner. Catching sight of her, he stopped, just staring for a long moment. When he finally spoke, his voice was husky and raw.

"Beautiful."

Monica looked down at the dress, pulling the train out and pretending to examine it closely. "It is beautiful, isn't it? Betsy tells me it was your mother's. I know I shouldn't wear it, but she insisted..." She knew she was rambling, and let the words trail off as he moved closer.

"It's perfect." Harley stood just in front of her and when she finally looked up, she found herself hypnotized by the soft, serious look in his eyes. He reached out to touch the beads just over her breasts, tracing the vine as it danced over her chest. She inhaled deeply then exhaled, his fingers sliding over the fabric to touch her warm bare skin. Her pulse raced under them, and she took a tentative step forward.

Behind Harley, Betsy cleared her throat. "Sorry bro, you'll have to wait. The front gate just radioed down that a group of suits just arrived, demanding to see the owner. If they're the ones after your girl here, you might want to get this wedding started."

Monica stepped back, breaking contact so she could think. This was it. Time to tell him she couldn't go through with it. "I ca--"

"Come on," he said, grabbing her hand and pulling her toward the door. "It's time to get hitched."

Struggling to keep up with his long strides in the unfamiliar heels, Monica let him tug her out of the dressing room and back down the hall, through two large double doors on the right. She was practically jogging to keep up as they hurried down a wide aisle between rows of glossy white benches. Finally they stopped under a white trellis arch with what appeared to be real vines growing in and around it. A tall, clean-cut man dressed in black with a white collar stood before them with a small white satin pillow in his hand. Two small bows on top secured one gold ring each, and Monica looked up at Harley, stunned. He merely shrugged and turned back to the preacher, a slight smirk on his lips.

"And do you, Monica Burns take this man to be your lawfully wedded husband?"

She blinked, frozen with panic. She had to end this. Now.

A commotion behind them made her turn, panic becoming fear as she saw her father walk confidently through the door with his goons on either side. "What the hell is going on here?" His deep, commanding tone echoed off the chapel walls.

"I do," she said, just loudly enough for her own voice to carry. Something cold and metal slipped onto her ring finger, and she looked down to see a thick gold band not unlike what she would have picked out herself. Quickly she placed the other ring on Harley's hand, and the preacher continued.

"By the power vested in me by the state of Nevada, I hereby pronounce you man and wife. You may kiss the bride."

Chapter Four

You may kiss the bride.

At Ian's words, Harley leaned down to place a soft, chaste kiss on Monica's trembling lips, squeezing her hands in his. "We'll finish this later," he whispered, then straightened, pulling her behind him as he turned to face the man who'd so rudely interrupted. "My bride's father, I presume? I'm afraid you missed the ceremony, but I'm sure we could probably scare up some champagne if you want to celebrate with us." He smiled, enjoying how the man's face turned red, with purple veins popping up on his neck. Monica hadn't been kidding when she'd said he had a temper.

"I'm Stephen Burns, and that's my daughter behind you," the man said, leaning to the side for a glimpse of his daughter. "Monica, what is the meaning of this? Show yourself, girl."

Monica was still grasping Harley's hand, her grip so

tight he'd have marks from her nails. He wondered where else she'd leave marks, the thought making him wish they were anywhere but here. He regarded her father, tall and slender with nary a gray hair. Dressed in a sharp black suit and a colorful tie that probably cost more than the bike helmet Monica had trashed, he was an imposing figure. He wasn't going to be happy when he went home empty handed, and it didn't look like he was going to go easy from the two burly guys standing just inside the chapel doors. Glancing over his shoulder he winked at Monica, struggling not to react to her snow-white face. He held out her hand to the minister.

"Ian, I think *my wife* is a bit overwhelmed. Would you show her to the back while I introduce myself to my new father-in-law?" Ian nodded, taking Monica's hand and pulling her gently toward a small door behind the altar. There was a back door from the minister's quarters, and hopefully Ian could sneak her out before anyone thought to check. Harley waited until the door closed, then descended the stairs to address his nemesis.

"Harlan Majors, owner of Fantasy Ranch and your new son-in-law. It's a pleasure to meet you, sir." He held out his hand, somehow keeping a pleasant smile pasted to his lips. "You can call me Harley." He waited, eyes locked on the other man's in a tense, powerful stare. Knowing he couldn't back down, he held firm, confident that Mr. Burns would rise to the challenge of being civilized.

After several long moments, strong fingers wrapped around his in a crushing grip. "I can't say it's a pleasure," Burns said, a grudging note of respect in his voice. "But we'll see. You own this whole compound?" He released Harley's hand, glancing around the room.

"We prefer to call it an adult theme park, but yes."

Burns motioned slightly to his guards and they walked out without a word, leaving them alone.

Harley decided to be hospitable. "I'd be happy to have someone give you a tour if you'd like. I think you'll find we put a lot of work into making fantasy a reality."

Burns nodded, running his fingers over the back of a pristine white pew. "I take it you're doing well then?"

"We do okay." Harley frowned as he watched Burns sit in the front row, an unconcerned smile on his face. "I'm sure your daughter will be happy here."

Burns chuckled, sending a chill through Harley. "Perhaps she would have. Unfortunately, she has a contract to fulfill, and I'm afraid I can't allow her to stay. My business is too important for a mere female to derail." The door opened at the back of the room, and one of Burns' men stepped in, nodding once. "Ah," Burns said, rising. "There's my ride. I wish I could stay longer, but I'm afraid I have important things to attend to. You'll excuse me?"

"You sonofabitch." Harley sprinted behind the altar and slammed the office door open then ran through the empty room to the back exit and out into the alley. A woman's cries for help rang out through the crisp night air, and he took off around the corner and through the graveyard. He reached the main road just in time to see Ian on the ground with Betsy bending over him, and a dark limo pulling away from the curb, Monica's hands pressed against the back side window.

* * *

Harley pulled his cell phone out and speed dialed his security team. "There's a limo headed for the front gate - stop it. And we need medical to the chapel. Ian's been hurt." Disconnecting, he tried to ignore the primal need to go reclaim his woman immediately and knelt beside his sister, who was helping the minister sit up. "What happened," he asked, pulling Ian to his feet. "How did they get Monica?"

"They knew," Ian said, wincing and holding a hand across his midsection as he straightened. "Those bodyguards were waiting in the alley when we came out. Monica fought hard, and I chased them, but one of them clocked me in the stomach. I'm sorry, Harlan - I couldn't hold them off."

Harley shook his head. "It's not your fault - he had it all planned out before he came in. He must have done his homework, but he's not getting past that gate." His phone buzzed and he glanced down, then grinned. "Security's got them now, it seems. Are you going to be okay? Medical's on the way, and Betsy can stay with you until they get here."

"I'll be fine." Ian took a tentative step forward. "What are you going to do?" He didn't look at Betsy and Harley wondered what she'd done this time. He'd have to have another talk with her about leaving his friend alone apparently. She'd been after Ian since they were kids and it was past time she gave up her childhood crush. But there were bigger issues to resolve at the moment.

He put his hands in his pockets, exhaling slowly. "I'm going to tell Burns to leave. Then I'll take Monica home."

"And you think he'll go along with that?"

Harley shrugged, grinning as he started to walk away. "He doesn't have a choice." He glanced back, noted Ian's uncomfortable glance at Betsy and took pity on the man. "Hey sis, wanna come with? Monica might need a friendly shoulder while I'm dealing with her dad."

Ian stood taller. "Go ahead, I'm fine. She needs you." Betsy stared at him, locked in some silent debate for a moment before she turned on her stilettos and joined Harley on the dirt road. As they walked, Harley wondered how long she'd be able to stay quiet. It turned out to be about ten feet.

"I saw the way you looked at her, you know. The way you touched her. You didn't marry her just to protect her." Her tone was confident, and despite the fact that he did feel...something for his new wife, it wasn't something he wanted to discuss with his sister.

He stared straight ahead, watching people swarm around the entrance gate where he assumed Burns was giving his team a hard time. His men were the best in the business though - you couldn't run a place like this without top-notch security to keep people from getting hurt.

"None of your business, sis. But since you opened the topic, what did you do to Ian? He's all nervous around you again - didn't I warn you to step back?"

She punched him in the arm. Hard. "I was just having a little fun with him," she said, a pout evident in her voice. "He needs to lighten up and you know it. It's not like we haven't known each other forever."

"He doesn't want you, Sis. I know it's hard to hear, and even harder to understand, but you've got to leave him alone. I hate to see you waiting on a guy who--"

"Hey!" A shout from up ahead pulled his attention back to the melee. "Come back here!" A figure broke free from the crowd and ran toward their position in the street.

"Is that Monica?" Betsy squinted into the dark.

Harley took in the figure, his eyes raking over every curve of the silhouette. It was definitely her - but how

had she gotten away? As she drew closer she turned
to look over her shoulder and he reached out to hook
an arm around her waist, pulling her close to him. She
panicked, punching and kicking at him with glazed
eyes. He squeezed her to mute her actions and bent
so his lips were close to her ear. "Monica, stop.
You're safe."

At his voice, she immediately stilled, gripping his
shoulders tightly. "Don't let him take me away -
please. You promised, remember? I can't--"

"No one's taking you anywhere you don't want to
go." He breathed in her scent, wondering how she
could still smell so sweet under the sweat and worry
she'd been through tonight. Knowing he still had to
deal with her father, he stepped back, holding her
arms when she would have followed him. "I have to
go," he said, regretting the fear that came into her
eyes. "Betsy's going to take you to my house. You'll
be safe there - he doesn't know where it is."

Monica shook her head, trying to pull out of his
grasp. "No. He won't listen to you - you can't stop
him. I have to get away..."

"You are away, hon." Betsy stepped in, curving an
arm around Monica's shoulders and meeting Harley's
eye with a slight nod. "You just let my big brother go
handle this for you. I know your dad's strong, but
Harley here, he's stronger and tougher. He'll take care
of you, but he needs to know you're safe." She pulled
Monica out of his grip, and Harley watched as Monica

looked his sister in the eye, then turned back to pin him with an anxious stare.

"I don't know what to do," she said in a low, even tone. "I want to trust you..."

He glanced over her shoulder. Time was running out. Who knows what other tricks Mr. Burns had up his sleeve? "Just give me a chance," he said, leaning down to place a light kiss on her lips. "If I'm not back in an hour, Betsy will help you get off the ranch without being seen. I promise you'll be safe, no matter what happens."

"One hour," she said, reaching a hand out as if to touch him, then pulling it back. "I--be careful." She turned to Betsy and followed the other woman into a nearby alley, both figures quickly disappearing in the darkness. Exhaling slowly, Harley strode up the street to make sure his lawyers had something to do tomorrow.

* * *

Fighting the urge to look back, Monica allowed Betsy to pull her between two buildings and down another side street. She wondered what time it was, and automatically looked down at her bare wrist. Saloon girls didn't wear watches. Had it only been hours since Braden had found her? It felt like a lifetime, and a sudden weariness seeped into her bones, slowing her pace with each step. The long train of her gown

was draped over her arm, and it felt like it weighed a
million pounds.

"Hey, are you okay?" Betsy's voice startled Monica,
and she looked up, surprised at the concern wrinkling
the other woman's brow. Why did these people care
so much about someone they barely knew, she
wondered. She managed to lift her lips in what she
hoped looked more like a smile than a grimace.

"Fine - I'm fine. I think it just finally hit me how
tired I am." She forced herself to move a little faster,
hoping it wasn't far. Her head was starting to spin a
little, and it would be nice to sit down for a few
minutes.

Betsy grasped her hand a little more tightly, tugging
her forward. "We're almost there..."

Monica resisted the urge to count the steps as she
followed Harley's sister up what looked to be a
marble staircase. As they reached the top she finally
looked up and stopped, blinking as she tried to take in
the enormous mansion before her. Betsy grinned and
pulled her toward the heavy wooden door. The slab
swung inward and they stepped through the opening
into a large, lavish entry hall with burgundy carpet,
black brocade walls, and a huge bouquet of fresh
flowers on the round table in the center.

"Welcome home, sis."

Monica stood, slowly turning her head from left to
right as she tried to take it all in. Between the dark
walls and under a large cut-glass chandelier a massive

double staircase with dark wood railings dominated the room. "You live here? For real?"

Betsy giggled, placing one hand on her hip and swept the other hand out in a dramatic curtsy. "Technically, I work here as a French maid for the guests. This particular building is set up to mimic a palace, where guests can pretend to be kings, queens, princesses - you name it. But there is a large suite at the end of each wing. I live in one, and Harley lives in the other. Come on, I'll show you."

She started walking toward the center of the stairs and Monica followed, curious when they kept going straight rather than up the steps. Betsy stopped in front of one of the walls and pushed on a small iron square with her thumb. A few seconds later, the wall slid open to reveal a small elevator car. Monica followed Betsy into the lift.

"The private residences are in the basement?"

The other woman nodded. "Harley thought it would be safer and easier to keep the guests from accidentally wandering in." The elevator stopped and they got out, Betsy leading the way down a long, narrow hall. "It's very nice though, you'll see. But first, I need to show you one other thing..." she turned to the left, and Monica was surprised to see another staircase leading down.

"Uh, just how far down does this go?" The stairs were a little steeper than the first set, and she held tight to the railing as she cautiously descended.

Betsy moved across a narrow landing to a heavy steel door and waited for Monica to catch up. "There's one more sub-floor beneath us, but this will do for now." She studied the rocks around the door for a moment, then reached between two for a smaller one they were hiding. Turning it over she retrieved a key and placed it in the lock. Waiting to open it, she glanced over her shoulder. "If you ever need to get off the ranch without anyone seeing you, this is one of the places you can go." She pulled the door open and the scent of wet, packed earth assaulted Monica's senses. Peering into the dark, she frowned.

"I'll need to remember a flashlight, I guess. Where does it go?"

Betsy chuckled, pointing to the left wall. Monica could just barely make out a small cooler on the ground just inside the entrance. "Everything you need should be in there - I check it monthly and try to keep the batteries fresh. There's also bottled water and a towel." She pushed the door shut again, making sure the lock engaged before she put the key back in its hiding spot. "The tunnel is long, but if you just keep going you'll eventually end up out by the highway. The entrance on that end is well-hidden too, so you'll have time to avoid whoever it is you're running from. Just stay in the main tunnel. If you turn off, it's easy to get lost. There are a lot of passages below the ranch from when it used to be a cult compound."

Monica nodded, the words barely registering as she

stared at the metal door. She should just go. She
could be gone before Harley got back. But Betsy was
already moving toward the stairs, expecting her to follow. She sighed and reached for the railing, pulling
herself up one step at a time. It wouldn't hurt to see
Harley's place, and she had to admit the underground
accommodations were intriguing. They reached the
top of the stairs and Betsy led her down the hall and
unlocked a door with her own key.

"Here we are," she said, pushing the door open and
leading the way inside. "The guest room is just down
that hall," she pointed to the right, "and there should
be something in the refrigerator - I just stocked it the
other day. Make yourself at home."

Smiling gratefully, Monica waited until Betsy had
gone and then locked the door and padded down the
hall to find the guest room. She felt completely
drained, and a nap sounded like the best option at this
point. She found a gigantic four-poster bed with a
green brocade canopy waiting, carefully laid the beautiful dress over a chair and crawled beneath the covers.

When she woke up, Harley was there, sitting beside
her on the bed with an amused smile on his face.

Monica stretched, keenly aware of Harley's gaze
slipping to her chest as her bare breasts threatened to

escape the bedspread.

"Have a good nap?" His rich, low voice slid like silk over her body and she struggled to hide her reaction. Adjusting the cover more tightly over her chest, she nodded.

"Do you always just walk into your guest's room without knocking?" She glared at him, pushing up on one elbow. Hoping he couldn't see her hardened nipples through the blanket.

He reached across to brace one hand at her back, effectively trapping her in place. "The guest room, no." The grin on his face vanished, replaced by a serious look that both scared and excited her. He bent down, until his nose was almost touching hers. "This is my bed though, and you are my wife. I didn't think the formalities were necessary."

Then his lips were on hers, his tongue demanding entrance as she rolled to her back and he followed. She reveled in his weight, the feel of his solid muscles under her touch and the earthy, all-male scent that filled her senses. Clearly he'd gone back on the no sex rule, and she was glad. Her whole body came alive at his touch as he drew the covers back and began to map her skin. His fingers traced over her chest then down one breast, kneading in increasingly smaller circles. Finding the pebbled tip, he pinched gently, pulling up and out and around in a way that sent electrical pulses down through her core. She whimpered as his fingers released her to be replaced with his mouth, his tongue swirling around the turgid peak. Arching up into him, she slid her hands down his chest and grasped his shirt, pulling it free of his waistband by the fistful.

"Too...many...clothes," she panted, reaching for the button on his jeans. He bit her nipple gently with one last tug, and then pushed up to slide off the bed to his feet. Making quick work of shedding his shirt, boots and pants, he pushed off his briefs, his erection springing free. Monica licked her lips at the size, not too long, but nice and thick. She was practically salivating at the thought of him in her mouth, and she moved to the edge of the bed as he stalked forward, her eyes trained on that delicious prize.

"Yum," she purred, reaching out with one hand as he drew near. Wrapping her fingers around his silky cock, she sucked him into her mouth. A growl erupted from somewhere deep in his throat, and he thrust forward, giving her what she wanted. She pulled back, lapping at the hard shaft then sucked just the tip in as she fondled his balls with her fingers. Legs shaking, he pulled away, placing his hands on her shoulders when she tried to follow.

"Darlin', you've got to stop now, or this show'll be over before it starts." He knelt in front of her, cupping her face in both hands and kissing her softly, warmly. She whimpered once more, her body aching for more.

He leaned back, his smile knowing as he stared into

her eyes for a long moment. "Sit up," he said in a raspy tone that belied his calm demeanor. She pushed up and swung her feet around, boldly opening her legs on each side of his shoulders.

"Like this?" She grinned coyly, not ashamed to ask for what she wanted. The look on his face told her he wanted the same thing, and she crooked a finger at him, inviting him closer even as she lowered her other hand to stroke her wet folds. He reached out to run a firm hand up the inside of each thigh, spreading them farther apart as he stroked higher, finally reaching her core. Holding her open he held her gaze as he licked a slow, wet trail between her legs and up to her sensitive nub.

Monica fell back on the bed, muscles quaking under his talented movements as she pinched and tugged at her nipples. Harley laved and suckled, bringing her just to the brink before abruptly pulling away. Bereft at the loss she arched her back, the crinkle of a foil packet sending a new flood of warmth through her center. Then finally, he was there, his cock probing at her entrance as he covered her with his body and kissed a path between her breasts to her neck. He bit down at the apex of her neck and shoulder, driving home in one hard thrust that sent a tantalizing shudder straight up through her spine.

"Oh!" She arched up again, pressing her breasts into his hard torso. The hard tips brushed through course hair, a wicked sensation as she met his thrusts with her own. He quickened his pace and she held on to his shoulders, a delicious fog settling over her brain as her release flirted just out of reach. Then he pressed hard on her clit and the orgasm spiraled through her just as he pressed in hard and growled out his own pleasure.

Harley laid his head on her chest, and she knew he must be able to hear how fast her heart was beating. She lay still, stroking his hair with one hand as they both tried to catch their breath. When he rolled away and padded to the bathroom, she restored order to the blankets, lifting them up for him as he joined her again. As he tucked her against his body, she snuggled against him, trying to keep her fears at bay for just a while longer.

Chapter Five

Harley woke several hours later to a soft, warm body tucked against him, a plump breast filling the palm of one hand. His body came to life as he remembered the events that had transpired earlier, and Monica shifted against him in her sleep, nestling her backside more firmly against his stiffening cock. Stifling a groan, he carefully moved his hand and began rolling to his back.

"Please," she whispered, her voice groggy with sleep. "Not yet."

Not sure whether she was awake or dreaming, he stilled for a moment and listened to her slow, even breathing. Moving slowly he got out of bed and tucked the covers in around her before heading to the ensuite bathroom for a shower. He stood under the lukewarm water, willing his body under control as he soaped up and rinsed off, trying to prepare for whatever would come next. He'd just wrapped a towel around his waist when a piercing scream sent him running back to the bedroom.

Monica flailed on the bed, her arms and legs tangled in the sheet as the bedspread fell to the floor. Thrashing her head back and forth she cried, her eyes tightly shut. "No! Please! I'm not ready...please not yet. Not him--let me go!"

Swearing under his breath he went to her side. "Monica, wake up." He hoped the loud, commanding tone would be enough to wake her, but she cried out again, rolling too close to the edge of the bed. Left with no choice, he grabbed her wrists, setting off a frantic fight response he regretted immediately. Holding tightly even though he knew she'd have bruises, he pulled her close, whispering softly into her ear. "Open your eyes, sweetheart. You're dreaming." He placed a light kiss a little lower on her neck as she stopped struggling, then leaned back, studying her face intently to make sure she was fully awake. Satisfied, he released her wrists, leaning back to give her some space. "Sorry about the grip - you were headed for a nasty fall."

She looked past him, her eyes widening as she rubbed her arms and scooted back a few inches. Glancing down at herself she seemed to realize she was naked, and he watched a pretty pink blush spread over her chest and up into her cheeks as she grabbed for the sheet, trying to cover herself. "Um...thanks," she said quietly, wiping her eyes though it looked as if she wasn't done crying yet. "Sorry about that - I get those sometimes."

"No need to apologize," Harley said, laying a hand over her thigh and stroking his thumb in what he hoped was a soothing back-and-forth motion. "Wanna talk about it?" He tensed up, waiting to hear what possibly could have happened to cause such violent nightmares. Then he was going to go break someone's neck.

Monica shook her head, surprising him again. "I'd rather not, if you don't mind." She glanced at his towel then looked quickly away, her shyness bringing a grin to his lips. "I could use a shower though, if you're done..."

"I've seen you naked, you know." He pulled the sheet away from her with a flick of the wrist. "And I'm not opposed to seeing a lot more of it." She hugged her knees to her chest, the sadness in her eyes replaced with a curious look.

"I thought you didn't want sex," she said, absently running a hand over the front of her calf. "Well, not with your wife, anyway. I take it you've changed your mind?"

Harley ran a hand through his hair, remembering his first proposal. Then he remembered her reaction. "You objected," he said, a knowing grin spreading over his face. "You wanted to sleep with me. Admit it."

"I never pretended otherwise," she said, her tone

matter-of-fact as she scooted closer to him on the bed. "But I was willing to go along with your rules since you seemed so set on them. And then you kissed me..."

He reached out, trailing a finger down her arm. "Yes I did. You were very convincing." He grasped her hand, pulling her to sit beside him on the edge of the bed. "You may have noticed I have a hard time resisting women..."

"All women?" She raised an eyebrow, the corners of her lips lifting the tiniest bit. "And here I thought I was special."

He laughed, pleased when her eyes followed his hands as he stood to readjust the towel at his waist. "I love women, sweetheart. That's why my lawyers were ready to marry me off. Less expensive staying with the same one, even if she does try to take my money." She was staring at him, both eyebrows raised now as he took the two steps back to the bed. He leaned over, his face just inches from hers and gazed into her pretty brown eyes. "But you're the only one I ever married, so that should count for something."

The urge to close the distance and kiss him was almost too strong to resist. Instead Monica leaned back and pulled a pillow across her lap, needing some sort of cover to make sure Harley's focus was on her words rather than her body.

"What exactly are you saying?" she asked, a shiver running through her skin. "Are we renegotiating the marriage contract?"

He shrugged, his expression thoughtful. "The damage is done as far as I'm concerned. We might as well enjoy ourselves for the rest of the year."

"Damage? Is that what we did? How on earth could having sex with me 'damage' you?" Monica swung her legs off the other side of the bed and grabbed a throw blanket off a chair near the window to wrap sarong-style around her body. She turned to face him, hands on her hips as he sat watching her from the bed. "You didn't honestly think that people would assume we weren't sleeping together after you married me..."

"I expected them to assume we were, actually." He stood, the towel at his waist slipping an inch lower on his hips. He didn't fix it. "But you don't want to be married and I don't really want anyone falling in love with me, so staying away from each other would have been the safer option." He crossed his arms over his chest, muscles flexing in a way that would have made her drool two minutes ago.

Now she was just mad. "So you think if I sleep with you, I'll fall in love with you. Just like that." She spied the bathroom door and walked toward it, stopping in the doorway to look over her shoulder at him. "Well screw you. Or not, in this case. Our original deal stands - no more sex." She stepped into the generous room and closed the door, reaching back to flip the lock before the tears started to fall.

"Monica?" He knocked on the door, twisting the knob back and forth. "Open the door, dammit."

She went to the shower and turned on the spray, then draped the blanket over an empty towel rack and stepped in. Letting the water run down her face she wept. Everything was such a mess. How had it gotten so complicated?

The answer was the same as it had always been. Her father. He was the reason she'd married Harley, and the reason she'd been running in the first place. And in all the personal drama, Harley hadn't told her how he'd dealt with her father, and suddenly she really needed to know. She used his shampoo to wash her hair, then quickly soaped and rinsed her body. Swearing under her breath when she remembered her lack of clothing, she wrapped the throw around herself again and cautiously opened the door. Relieved that no one was there, she padded over to the freshly made bed where she found a small stack of folded clothes and a note. Unfolding the paper, she scanned the lines.

"I hope these fit - they belong to my sister. I'll be waiting in the living room."

She pulled on her own bra and panties, which appeared to have been washed. Betsy had loaned her a super-soft pair of jeans that would work if she rolled them up, along with a fitted white cashmere sweater that clung in all the right places. Not half bad, she thought as she checked herself out in the freestanding mirror and fluffed her still-damp hair. Unable to wait any longer she retraced last night's route back to the front door, and turned to see Harley waiting for her on one of two plush overstuffed couches. He stood as she approached, his lips pressed into a thin line.

"What happened with my father last night?"

"Why don't you sit down?"

Monica almost protested on principle, but the serious look in those dark, brooding eyes convinced her otherwise. She chose a dark green overstuffed armchair, thinking as she sank into the plush cushions that it would make a wonderful spot to read under more favorable circumstances. Harley sat across from her on a matching sofa, perched on the edge with his forearms braced on his knees. She frowned.

"I'm sitting, now spill. Did something happen to my father? Is he okay?" She leaned forward, gripping the edge of the seat with her hands.

Harley shook his head. "He's fine," he said drawing out the words longer than necessary. "We came to an agreement of sorts, but you're not going to like it. And I'm already working on a way to get out of it, so don't overreact, okay?"

She threw her hands up and fell dramatically back against the chair. "An agreement? Of course. I sure know how to pick 'em, don't I?" Raising her head she settled more comfortably in the chair, wondering if she would be using that secret tunnel tonight after all. "Do tell, Harlan. What did you and my father decide about the rest of my life?"

Pushing his hands on his knees, he stood, pacing between the couch and the coffee table. "It turns out that your father owns the company that holds our mortgage to this place. When things got heated last night, he threatened to call in the note. I'm close to being able to pay it off, but just not quite there yet." He moved over to the cold, dark fireplace and propped one arm up on the mantle. "I didn't have any choice. It was either agree or lose the ranch. I can't lose this place, Monica. It's my life."

She nodded, her heart beating faster at his words. Stephen Burns was a powerful guy, and he'd been holding things over people's heads since she was just a child. Disappointing as it was to hear, his treatment of Harley wasn't really surprising. "It's obviously something pretty bad, so you might as well get it over with." She reached out as he paced close and took his hand, pulling him to sit on the large ottoman in front of her. "We'll figure out a way to deal with it."

"It's two things, really," he said, his voice low with that raspy quality she found so sexy. "First, I have to transport packages to one of his offices in Reno. He'll have one dropped off here twice a month."

Monica's frown deepened. "What's in the package?" she asked, even though she wasn't sure she wanted to know.

"Drugs or cash is my guess. I'm not supposed to look or ask questions."

She nodded, oddly energized by the possibility of seeing just what her father wanted moved. It could be something they could use as leverage later. "And the second?"

"He wants grandchildren, Monica. A boy and a girl at least two years old before we can divorce, or he'll take the ranch away."

* * *

Monica released her grip on his arm like it was a hot pan, pulling as far away from him as she could get within the confines of the chair. "No," she said, her arms crossed over her chest. "No. I'm not having kids, ever. So he can just go straight to hell. Straight. To. Hell."

She was trembling, hot red anger rising in her face. Harley was glad he'd decided not to tell her the rest for now. He'd known she'd react badly, but this was far more dramatic than expected. He wondered if she knew more about her father's criminal activities than she let on.

"Do you want to talk about it?" he said softly, reaching out to lay one hand on her knee.

She brushed it aside, launching herself out the chair and slipping past before he could blink. "There's nothing to talk about, I just don't want kids." She walked over to the fireplace then turned suddenly, her intense gaze burning into him. "You said you had a plan?"

He nodded. "Like I said, I've almost got enough saved up to pay off the ranch. I say we play along for six months. Then when I've got the money, we trade the ranch for our silence and your freedom."

"It seems too simple." She frowned, shaking her head. "I just don't know...something's off about all of this. Why didn't he just call in the note? Why play with us like this? It doesn't make any sense."

Harley felt a twinge of guilt as he watched her pace with furrowed brow, trying to make one plus one equal three. Burns had no intention of ever giving up the ranch - he was certain of that. Harley had been about to tell him just where he could stick his demands regardless of the consequences when one of Burns' bodyguards had interrupted them with a call. Burns stepped out of the room to answer it, and the bodyguard left behind had identified himself as undercover FBI agent Austin Daniels. He'd asked Harley to play along and find out exactly what was in those *packages*. The FBI suspected he was abducting and smuggling women out of the country to sell as sex slaves, but he normally stayed far enough away from the day-to-day operations that Daniels hadn't been able to connect him to it. Yet.

He wanted Harley to confirm his suspicions and collect any evidence that might connect Burns to the smuggling ring. Since Monica was at the ranch there was a possibility that Burns would spend more time there now, having expressed an interest in getting to know his daughter better again. If he happened to oversee a hand-off or two, that would go a long way toward putting him behind bars.

Daniels had assured him the ranch would be turned over free and clear after Burns was taken into custody, and Harley had reluctantly agreed. He hadn't really seen a choice, since any legal proceedings against Burns at this point could close down the ranch for months or even years, and this way they had a chance to get Monica's father out of her life forever. Not to mention the women, if that was indeed what Burns was smuggling.

He stood up, meeting Monica's troubled gaze. "I don't know, sweetheart. But like I said before, I'm working on a way to get us out of this mess, and get your father out of your life for good, if that's what you want."

She nodded, slowly. "What do we do now?"

A loud buzzing from Harley's pocket filled the space between them, and he dug his phone out of his pocket to answer. He listened intently to the frantic voice on the other end, feeling her tension surround him as she watched and waited. "Just hang on a few more minutes, if you can. We'll be right there," he said and disconnected the call. She raised her eyebrows, and he grinned.

"Ready to play the wench again, darlin'?"

Chapter Six

"Saloon girl," Monica corrected automatically, guilt edging in as she remembered she had been scheduled to work this morning. It hadn't mattered when she'd thought she wasn't coming back. "Just let me change..." She turned to go, halted by warm fingers closed lightly around her upper arm. Looking up, she met his concerned gaze.

"Are you sure you're up for this? I could call someone else instead."

Swallowing hard, she nodded. "It will be good to do something mundane for awhile. Everything's been so...intense," she said, pulling gently out of his grasp. "I could use the break."

He nodded, stepping aside. "I'll take you down on the four-wheeler. I have some things to get done this afternoon, but I'll be back in time to bring you home."

"Thanks." She went down the hall to her - *his* room, and after a brief search found the costume hanging in the closet right next to all of his things. Whoever had washed her under things must have cleaned it too, and she was grateful. Shimmying out of the jeans and shirt she'd put on just under an hour ago, she dressed quickly then used the bathroom mirror to fluff her drying hair. As she lowered her hand, a glint of gold flashed in the mirror, and she looked down to examine the ring Harley had given her. It was probably the most symbolic thing she'd ever owned, and yet it seemed to mock her from its place on her finger.

Staring into her own eyes, she waited for the urge to run, the one she would have listened to last night if she hadn't been so tired. She held up her left hand, wiggled it in the mirror to remind herself she was well and truly married. Trapped. Caged, even if it was only supposed to be short term.

Nothing.

Fear prickled under her skin as she contemplated what that meant. She couldn't afford to be comfortable, to settle down. To trust. This feeling of belonging couldn't be real, she wouldn't let it. Belonging to someone - with someone - always ended badly.

She went back to the bedroom and laced her feet into the tall leather boots, then went to find Harley, skirt swishing around her ankles. As she neared the kitchen, the sound of his voice drifted through the doorway.

"No, Burns specifically said not to use a room near his. Use three-twelve. It should be clean and empty. I'll be there in about 20 minutes."

Monica entered in time to see him hang up the phone, and shot him a questioning look. "My father is still here?"

"Only for tonight," Harley said, looking her up and down. "Nice," he said, a grin playing at his lips. "Very nice."

She shook her head, trying to hold back a smile. "Don't even go there," she said, following him to the front door. "Why is my father still here?"

Harley pulled the door shut behind them, his expression stiff as he walked past her down a long, undecorated hall. "Apparently he booked a dinner party here at the mansion for tonight before he knew you were here," he said, leading the way to a small bank of elevators and pushing the call button. "Some conference his company was hosting in Reno. That's why your ex was here too - he skipped out on a couple meetings to scout out our security ahead of time. It was just chance that he decided on the saloon to drink in that night instead of the Double D."

"He's not my ex." Monica stepped onto the elevator, only vaguely remembering having been on it the night before. "I guess he was bound to find me anyways then, from the sounds of it. The universe is trying to tell me something. Maybe I should have just gone--"

Harley pushed the hold button and the elevator jerked to a stop. Wary, Monica backed away as he advanced, until her shoulders were pressed into the corner. Heat radiated off his body as he braced his forearms on either side of her head and leaned in. "The universe isn't telling you anything. Common sense is telling you it's time to quit running and fight back, so fight, damn it! Don't let him or anyone else tell you how to live your life." He leaned closer, his breath hot on her face and she knew in another second, he'd be kissing her. And she wouldn't be able to resist.

His muscles flexed instinctively under her hands as she looked him in the eye and pushed him away. "That's rich coming from someone who lives his life on the advice of his lawyers."

Harley stared at her for a long moment and then pushed the button to start the elevator again. "I listen to my lawyers when they give good advice - and I pay them to give good advice," he said, crossing his arms over his chest. "But they don't run my life. I'm sure there are at least a dozen women out there they would have preferred I married instead of you." The doors opened and he walked out without so much as a backward glance.

Monica followed, practically jogging to catch up as he strode through the back half of the mansion. She'd succeeded in pushing him away but it hurt to know she'd hurt him. Biting back the apology on her lips, she swung onto the seat of the four-wheeler behind him and held on as he turned over the engine. She could feel the disapproval coming off him in waves and wondered if this was what her life would be like from now on.

A minute later, he pulled up outside the saloon, not bothering to turn off the engine. She got off the machine, resisting the urge to glance at him before walking away. She'd only taken a step when strong fingers circled her wrist and pulled her off-balance. She stumbled back against him, at his mercy as he pulled her across his lap and against his chest, lowered his head and seared her lips in a strong, branding kiss.

As quickly as it had started, it was over, and without looking directly at her he set her on her feet and gunned the engine. She watched him drive away, her body shaking at the powerful emotions warring inside her. Taking a deep breath, she exhaled slowly, composing herself as much as she could before she went inside.

* * *

Several hours later, Monica took a seat at a back table, her shift almost over. She sipped a soda and watched the last of the patrons packing up to leave, finally allowing herself to think about that kiss. Harley had been hungry, desperate - she had felt it all the way to her toes even in the few seconds before he'd left her. Thinking back, she revisited every expression, every nuance from the conversations they'd had. He hadn't once suggested she leave. Hadn't even blamed her for all the trouble he was facing now, when most men would be railing at her or tossing her out on her ear. Why? The only possible answer both scared her to her core, and excited her like nothing ever had. Could it be that he really cared for her?

She checked her watch. It was just past six and the mansion was probably being prepared for her father's dinner party. She had no desire to run into him or his cronies tonight, but she'd slip in the back door they'd used that morning and find her way down to Harley's suite without being seen. First though, she wanted to stop by her old room. She'd left in hurry the night before and wanted to make sure she hadn't left anything.

An engine roared outside and she looked out in time to see Harley on the four-wheeler, remembering what he'd said earlier about taking her home. Not ready to deal with him again just yet, she quickly made her way down the back hall again, just as she had the night before. Slipping out the back door, she ran down the alley toward the main entrance to the ranch, took a left and went past the medieval-looking castle to the large building just beyond that served as a dorm for the staff.

After she'd checked her room on the fifth floor,

she went out the side door and around the castle to
the VIP Hotel. Entering the lobby, she stopped short
when she heard her father's voice from around a
corner.

"Three-twelve," he said, pausing for a long moment. "That's correct. The clients will be waiting at
the address in Reno tomorrow. Don't be late." A
short high beep signaled that he'd disconnected the
call. Monica waited until she heard the elevator doors
open and close before she peeked around the corner
at the now-empty corridor.

Three-twelve. That was the room number Harley
had said on the phone that morning, she was sure of
it. The first package must be here, but why hadn't he
told her? So much for working together.

She walked to the stairwell and went up three
floors, then slowly opened the door, looking both
ways down the hall before she entered. Moving
quickly, she found room three-twelve on the other
side of the building. Unsure of what to do next, she
found a hiding spot behind a tall fake plant in a small
alcove twenty feet away, and settled in to wait.

* * *

Twenty minutes later, Monica's feet were numb.
She stretched them gingerly, wincing at the sharp
prickling sensations that shot through her ankles as
circulation returned. She needed to get back - Harley

would be wondering where she was, a thought that both scared her and gave her an unfamiliar sense of belonging that she wasn't quite sure she liked.

Peeking out carefully through the fake branches she scanned the hallway, listening for any noise that might indicate that someone was coming. Hearing and seeing nothing, she eased out of the alcove and walked toward room three-twelve. She'd go past just one time, and then be on her way. Maybe Harley would bring her back tomorrow if she asked nicely.

Just ahead a door opened on the right and she froze. Male voices rumbled into the silence along with a softer, mewling sound that made her frown. Animals weren't allowed in the building. Had someone been keeping a cat in their room?

A tall man stepped into the hall and Monica instinctively lowered her head, letting her hair fall across her face. Trying to appear as though she belonged there, she kept walking, forcing herself to maintain a normal pace instead of the sprint every muscle in her body was primed for. She walked past, noting the child carrier being passed to the man in the hall on her way by. Not a cat after all, but a baby, and a very young one at that. Odd, considering children weren't allowed at the ranch.

She heard the room door close as she reached the corner, and once around it she glanced back over her shoulder just in time to see the man and baby disappear into another room on the other side of the hall.

The same room she'd been watching for nearly half an hour.

Quickly she ran to the stairwell and hurried down to the first floor. Stepping out into the near-darkness, she took a few deep breaths and then walked casually between the buildings to the back of the mansion. She'd slip in the back, find Harley and tell him what she saw. He'd assigned the room this morning, so he had to know something about what was going on there.

Entering through the same door she'd left by that morning, Monica retraced her steps to the private elevator, realizing only when she reached the long hall in the basement that she didn't have a key to Harley's suite yet. She reached the door, thinking to look around for a spare key that might be hidden when the door swung open. Startled, she gasped, his silhouette stark and imposing against the light coming from behind him.

"Where the hell have you been?" He reached out and grabbed her wrist, pulling her against him as he slammed the door behind her. "Do you have any idea how long I've been looking for you? I can't protect you if I don't know where you are, Monica. When I tell you to wait for me, wait, dammit!" He locked his arms around her back and looked in to her eyes, the genuine worry reflected there belying his angry expression. He leaned in and covered her lips with a punishing kiss that inflamed both her body and her pride.

She pushed at his chest, turning her head when he refused to release his hold. "You don't own me," she said, pushing at his chest. His arms only tightened around her and she struggled, needing to get away before her baser instincts took over. "Let me go! Just because we're married doesn't give you the right to man-handle me."

"That's not what you were saying last night, darlin'."

He let go abruptly and she stumbled backward into the wall. He crossed his arms over his chest, watching as she regained her balance. "I suppose you think this is funny," she said, brushing off her skirts and pushing her hair back.

He shrugged. "Not particularly. I do think this whole thing would go a lot better if you'd stop fighting me. Especially since I've put my whole livelihood on the line for you. You could show a little respect."

"No one asked you to put yourself out," Monica said, regretting the words even as she said them. He was right. He didn't have help her - he could have just handed her over and not gotten involved. He shook his head and turned toward the kitchen, walking away. As she stared at his retreating back, she knew that if she didn't do something, she'd lose whatever this thing between them was. In that moment, she realized it wasn't being with him that she was afraid of. It was losing the one person who truly seemed to care about her.

"Wait," she said quietly, relief flooding through her when he stopped, not looking back, but not leaving. "I'm...sorry."

* * *

Monica's soft words tore at Harley's controlled facade. Forcing himself not to turn around, he kept his back to her until a tentative hand slid down his shoulder blade to the small of his back. Her touch was like a spark to the smoldering fire just underneath his skin, and when she came around to face him with wide, fearful eyes he couldn't hold back any longer.

Grabbing her arms he hauled her up against him, kissing her lips, her jaw, her forehead, her neck. Her scent intoxicated him, warm and sweet even though the scent of stale beer lingered in the background. She shuddered as he suckled the spot where her neck and shoulder met, her hands sliding up his chest to the top button of his shirt. Exploring her smooth skin inch by inch, he slowly worked lower, tracing the low-cut neckline down to where her cleavage began. Reaching behind the thin fabric he lifted one perfect breast, running his thumb over the taunt peak several times before he moved to the other. Suckling both briefly, he straightened, moving half-a-step back as she slid his shirt off his shoulders and down his arms.

"You're beautiful like that," he said, staring at her

lovely round globes supported by the snug corset and framed by the edges of her shirt collar. Raising his stare he looked into her eyes, glassy with arousal. "I'll accept your apology on two conditions," he said, cupping the side of her face with one hand. "First, you stop fighting me. If we're gonna get through this and beat your father at his own game, we need to work as a team. No more running off, no secrets. Agreed?"

She nodded. "Agreed. And the second?"

He let his fingers drift down her neck, across her chest and over each breast in turn, rolling the pert tips between his thumb and forefinger. "On your knees, wench."

Harley could tell his words chafed, but he merely raised his eyebrows as she stared up at him. He knew the only reason she was resisting was because it had been a demand rather than a request. Judging from the flush of her skin and those huge, dilated eyes, she wanted it just as much as he did. But did she want it bad enough?

Slowly she eased down in front of him, reaching out to unsnap his jeans. He nearly sighed in relief when she unzipped his pants and took him in hand. Leaning forward, she slowly ran her tongue over the tight flesh then looked up at him as she sucked him into her mouth. The sight of her pretty lips framing his cock sent heat spiraling through his balls, and he ran his fingers through her hair as she licked and bobbed, holding his gaze and driving him wild. So beautiful.

Her hands smoothed over his thighs, light, tickling, and she closed her eyes, shutting him out. He felt the loss keenly, wishing she'd give him - *them,* a chance. But she wouldn't let herself stay. Wouldn't let herself be happy with him. He growled low, pulling away from her sweet mouth and pulling her to her feet. Pressing a quick, hard kiss to her neck, he spun her around and bent her over, tossing her skirt over her back as she used the wall for support. She widened her stance in silent invitation and he pulled the scrap of fabric between her legs aside, plunging into her warm, wet heat. Grabbing her hips, he thrust in and out, over and over, pushing her against the wall as he took out his frustration between her legs.

The tension rose between his legs, and he leaned over, one hand sliding down to find the sensitive nub between her legs. He moved his finger in tiny circles, increasing the pressure until she cried out, grinding her luscious bottom against his groin. He thrust once, again, then pressed hard between her legs as he came hard, his semen coating her inner passage.

"Fuck." He quickly pulled out, stumbling backward in his haste. "I'm sorry...I..."

Chapter Seven

Monica kept her hands on the wall to steady herself, straightening on shaky legs. Harley cussed a few more times under his breath, and she straightened her skirt, knowing she should do...something, but not wanting to just walk away. She knew he hadn't forgotten the condom on purpose, but there wasn't really anything to say. It wasn't okay, and she found herself shaking at the thought of what could happen. She needed to get away.

Clearing her throat, she forced herself to look at him. Braced for anger, she was unprepared for the raw fear and anguish reflected in his face. Fighting the urge to reach out and pull him into her arms, she swallowed hard. "I know you didn't mean to. It's not a good time anyway, so maybe nothing will happen. I...need a shower, if that's okay."

"Monica..." he reached for her, but she stepped

around him, walking quickly toward the bedroom. It
would be okay. It had to be.

Stepping into the shower she reached for the soap,
hesitating before she pressed it against her skin. His
scent clung to her, and as much as she didn't want to
be pregnant, she also didn't want to wash the early,
masculine scent away. She closed her eyes, breathing
in deeply before finally lathering ample suds over her
breasts, her stomach, and between her legs. She knew
there was no going back now, no way to take back
what had happened. But she did a thorough job anyway then stood underneath the hot stream, trying to
hold back the tears.

It was obvious from his reaction that Harley didn't
want her any longer than she had to stay, and who
could blame him? But she couldn't dwell on that now.
The only way to put an end to this and give him back
his freedom was to find out what her father was hiding, and put him away for good. Somehow she'd find
a way to pay Harley back for going through all this
with her - it was the least she could do.

Turning off the water she stepped out and wrapped
a towel around herself. Quickly dressing in the jeans
and sweater she'd worn earlier, she took a deep breath
and went to find Harley. In all the confusion, she
hadn't told him what she saw in the apartment building, and they needed to talk about what to do next.

She sensed the suite was empty as she walked
down the hall, but checked in all the main rooms just

in case. He must have gone back upstairs to her
father's company dinner - she'd forgotten he was supposed to attend in all the chaos. There was a shiny key
lying on the counter, with her name on a note underneath. Slipping it into her pocket, she let herself out,
determined to find him and tell him what she'd seen.

Half-way to the elevators, she heard a sound from
the other end of the hall. Betsy's apartment was that
way, and Monica decided to go thank her for the
clothes. As she got closer she could see the other woman's profile as she leaned against the wall, shoes in
hand. It sounded like she was crying.

"Betsy? Are you okay?" Monica asked, frowning at
the flushed skin and streaked mascara on Betsy's face
as Harley's sister nodded.

"I...yes," Betsy said with a nervous laugh, blinking
quickly. "Just some guy trouble. You know how men
are."

Monica nodded. "Yes I do," she said quietly.
"Come on, let's talk."

"It's kind of messy," Betsy said, sliding the key into
the door of her suite. I've been working extra shifts
lately, and--" She stopped abruptly, looking down at
the floor. "What's this?" Monica glanced down to see
a manila envelope with a brass clasp.

Monica shrugged. "Were you expecting
something?" Betsy turned the envelope over, but
there was no address.

"No," she said, bending the metal tabs up and lifting the flap. "I thought maybe you left it. No one else is supposed to be down here, not even the staff." She held it open and looked inside. Sliding out a single piece of paper, she stared at it for a long moment.

Monica reached for the page, gasping at the image of Betsy on it. Disturbing didn't really do justice to the photo - someone must really hate her. "Lock the-- wait, this was inside the door, right?" Betsy nodded, still stunned. "Come on," Monica said, grabbing her hand and tugging her quickly back out into the hall. She slammed the door behind them and pulled Betsy back down the hall. "Whoever left that could still be in there...we need to call Harley."

* * *

"Maybe it's just a practical joke," Betsy offered from a stool by the kitchen counter. She couldn't seem to look away from the image. Monica took the paper from her, turning it face down on the counter as she dialed Harley's number. Hopefully he wouldn't ignore the call when her number came up.

"Harley, it's me," she said as soon as she heard his wary greeting. "We have a serious problem - you need to come down here right away."

"I can't - I'm with your father. It will have to wait for later." His voice was low, and she frowned. Her father was just going to have to wait. His sister's life was in danger.

"Want me to talk to him?" Betsy said.

Monica shook her head, looking down at the floor. She took a deep breath. "Harlan Majors, get your ass down here right now. There's something you need to see." She disconnected the call and tossed her phone on the counter, letting out a long sigh as she rubbed her forehead, glancing at Betsy. "Was he always this pigheaded?"

Betsy met her gaze with a sympathetic look. "Worse, I'm afraid. He's always wanted to do exactly the opposite of what anyone tells him to do, which made for some interesting high school days." She grinned. "Not many people have the balls to talk to him like that though. I'll bet for you, he's on his way down."

Right on cue, the front door opened and then slammed shut. Harley came around the corner two seconds later, a scowl on his face as he glanced from one woman to the other. Finally he focused on Monica, his jaw tight. "What the hell is going on? Why didn't you tell me Betsy was here?" The venom in his voice surprised her. She'd thought he would calm down once he saw his sister, but it seemed to be making things worse. He turned to Betsy, his voice softening slightly. "Ian called just before Monica. He left a message saying Derek might be here at the ranch. Is that true? Why didn't you tell me he was out of jail?"

Monica struggled to keep a neutral expression,

watching as Betsy shook her head, blinking hard. "I was going to tell you about Derek, but you've been so busy with getting married and all - I didn't want to distract you. Then I thought I saw him tonight and sort of freaked out, so I went to Ian's but we had a fight and I came home and that's when I found this." She flipped the paper over and slid it in front of him. "Monica was with me and wanted to call you so here we are."

Harley stared down at the image, his phone jangling from his pocket. Without taking his eyes off the page, he held the phone up to his ear and answered with a terse, "Yeah."

Monica glanced down at the photo again. It was a picture of Betsy, taken recently in the same French maid outfit she still had on, so whoever had gotten it either was here or had been. Whoever left it had photo-shopped her image with a noose around her neck, hanging from the banister of the grand double staircase on the main floor. Her wrists looked like they'd been slit, and her blood pooled on the floor below. Monica tried to imagine what it would be like if it was her in the photo, and couldn't. Whoever had done this was one sick individual. She shivered at the thought that he might be here at the ranch.

"We're all in my suite, Ian...come on over." Harley disconnected the call, and shoved the phone down in his front pocket. Looking thoughtfully at Betsy, he reached across the counter and took one of her hands. "He sounds pretty bad, sis - what were you fighting about? Did you hit on him again?"

Monica felt bad for the other woman as she squirmed on the seat, avoiding Harley's gaze. "I'm sure it doesn't matter," she said, earning a grateful look from Betsy, and a scowl from Harley. "Whatever the problem, I'm sure they'll get over it."

Harley shook his head, a chuckle of disbelief escaping. "Darlin', you don't know what you're talking about. Why don't you run upstairs and make sure *our guest* isn't foaming at the mouth because I'm not there. I'll be up as soon as I'm done here."

* * *

For a moment, Monica couldn't move. Could barely breathe as anger hit hard and fast. Had Harley really just dismissed her like a misbehaving child? She searched for words, some statement that would adequately express her feelings, but shock and disbelief had frozen her vocabulary.

"Harlan Majors." Betsy's stern voice broke through Monica's brain fog, and she blinked. Apparently the disappointed tone had gotten through to Harley too, his expression softening. He reached out to her, but she shrugged away from his touch. Not trusting herself to speak around the lump in her throat, she turned and ran out of the suite. He didn't want her around? Fine. She'd check in on her father, and then she was going back to the dorm to find out what was going on in room three-twelve. If she could get the information needed to put her father away, she could end this whole thing once and for all.

Jabbing at the elevator call button, she swiped a tear from her cheek with the other hand. Her muscles tensed at the sound of footsteps coming from the direction of Betsy's apartment. She pressed against the wall in a dark corner, hoping whoever it was would walk right past. When the minister who had performed the wedding ceremony strode by, she exhaled long and slow. Ian must have gone to Betsy's first, and then called Harley. The elevator doors opened and she stepped inside, steeling herself to see her father again.

* * *

Harley watched Monica go, wondering if he'd ever see her again. He knew he should go after her, but he couldn't leave Betsy here alone. Not with the possibility of her ex running around.

"You should go after her," Betsy said, echoing his thoughts. "That was uncalled for and you know it. She just wanted to help."

He turned to meet her reproachful gaze. "I'll talk to her later. Your safety is more important right now." He fought the urge to look over his shoulder when he heard the front door open and close. "When did

Derek get out of prison?"

"A couple weeks ago. Look, I know I should have told you, but--" she stopped, looking over his shoulder. He turned, nodding to Ian who was standing in the doorway. His jaw was set, his expression stern, but that sad, longing look in his eyes he always wore around Betsy was still very much intact.

"Ian," Harley said, holding out his hand. The minister gripped it then turned to Betsy, whose face had suddenly gone beet red. Harley reached across the counter and slid the photo to his friend. "Someone left this under her door this morning. We need to get her out of here, at least until I can figure out what's going on with Derek."

The minister nodded. "I offered to loan her the money, but she refused. I was hoping you could talk some sense into her." He grabbed the photo and flipped it over with a sneer.

"I don't want to go anywhere," Betsy said quietly, her eyes on the stone counter top. "If I run, he wins."

"If you run, you stay alive," Harley countered. "I've got all sorts of crap going on here right now and Derek is just one more thing. I'll find him, and I'll make sure he doesn't bother you again, but you have to get out of here so I won't be worried about you every second of the day." He looked at Ian. His friend had said repeatedly that he wasn't interested in anything with Betsy, but the concern in his eyes seemed like more than just friendly concern to Harley. Maybe a week alone together would decide the issue once and for all. An image of Monica's stricken face flashed in his head and he wished they could have a week together, just the two of them. He needed to go find her. Now.

He curled a hand over Ian's shoulder. "I need you to take her away from here. I don't care where, and I don't need to know, just find somewhere safe to hole up for a week or so. Charge it to the ranch. Just keep her safe."

"But I--" Betsy stood up, her eyes flashing fire.

Harley held his hand up, giving her a stern look. "He's the only one I trust to take care of you, sis. Don't argue. Just go." He walked around the counter and gave her a quick hug, then headed for the door, pausing to glance back over his shoulder. "Don't give him any trouble, Bets. This is serious." Without waiting for an answer, he walked out. With any luck, he could catch Monica to apologize before she left.

Chapter Eight

When he reached the main floor, Harley took a
right just beyond the stairs and followed a narrow hall
to the end where it opened into a large, dark parlor.
Candles in antique wall sconces dimly lit the crowded
room where the dinner party guests were mingling
and enjoying small glasses of sherry and port. He
chose a spot along the wall just inside the doorway
and scanned the crowd, hoping for a glimpse of Monica's long, curly hair. Twice he thought he saw her,
but the face didn't match the hair. Then he spotted
Stephen Burns near a window across the room, and
made his way through the crowd to stand beside his
new father-in-law. It was all he could do not to immediately ask about Monica.

"Mr. Burns. I trust everything is going well this
evening?"

The older man nodded thoughtfully, taking a small

sip of the dark amber liquid in his glass. "Well enough, well enough. I couldn't help but notice you disappeared - is everything okay?" The hint of disapproval made Harley bristle, but he worked to maintain a bored look.

"Just a family tiff," he said, glancing at faces walking past and wondering if Derek was still here. "I handled it. Speaking of family, did Monica come see you?"

He could see his words hit the intended mark as Burns blinked, the lines on his face hardening. Apparently he didn't care for being reminded that they were family now. That fact gave Harley a great deal of pleasure, and he was hard-pressed to stifle a laugh.

"She was here briefly," Burns replied. "Said you asked her to check on me, and that she had some things to do down at the saloon. She didn't look happy, son. I'd suggest you--"

Harley held up a hand, his gaze fixed on a figure walking toward the door. Betsy was right - Derek was here at the ranch. "Hold that thought," he told Burns. "There's something I need to go do." Without giving the man a chance to respond, he shouldered his way through the crowd and intercepted Derek just as he stepped into the hall.

"What the hell are you doing on my ranch, Wilson." The man grinned, his thin lips stretched too tight on the left against a scar that spanned his jaw line. Harley felt a moment of satisfaction knowing that his baby sister had put that mark there.

"Just taking care of some unfinished business, Majors. Lucky thing I ran into Mr. Burns in Reno the other day. He told me all about this place, and how the man who runs it just married his daughter. Wasn't real happy about it, if I recall. If I hadn't heard your name, probably never would have found you." He nodded as though pleased with himself, thumbs tucked casually into the front pockets of his weathered jeans. Frowning thoughtfully, he cocked his head to the side. "So how is your sister these days, Majors? Still breaking hearts and heads?"

Ignoring his better judgment, Harley swung back and sent his fist into Derek's face, pain exploding through his hand and spidering up his arm. Caught completely off guard, the other man hit the wall hard, his head bouncing off the dark brocade fabric before he sprawled on the floor between two antique chairs.

Harley opened his fist, wincing as he flexed his fingers to make sure nothing was broken. The din from the crowd had grown quieter, and he glanced over at the crowd looking on in horror. Burns stepped out of the mass and came to stand beside Harley, looking thoughtfully down at Derek's bloodied visage.

"Well son, looks like you've met Mr. Wilson. And from what I see, it's probably a good thing he was just leaving." He lifted one finger, and two of his bodyguards separated from the crowd. They went to Derek and picked him up, carrying him down the hall toward the door. Burns turned to the crowd, a smile on his lips. "Show's over, folks. Enjoy the rest of your night."

The din of murmured conversation rose quickly, and Harley stood in the hallway, anxious to make his escape. He glanced at Monica's father, then back down the hall. "Derek Wilson isn't welcome here, sir, and I'll send him back to jail in a heartbeat if he's not off my property in thirty minutes. Just so we're clear."

"Fine." Burns nodded, a glimmer of respect in his eyes. "My men will escort him into town and drop him off at the nearest hospital. Mind telling me what he did to get you all riled up?"

"It's personal. Now if you don't mind, I need to go--"

"Whatever it is will have to wait. I need you to go deliver a package. It's in room three-twelve, just like we agreed, and should be delivered to this address." Burns took a folded slip of paper out of his pocket and handed it to Harley. "There's a courier with the package - you're just the driver. After the transaction is complete, bring the courier back."

Harley looked down at the note. Beneath the scrawled address it said "11pm, sharp." He checked his watch, it was already ten, and it would take at least thirty minutes to reach Reno. They'd barely make it in time if he left right now for the dorms. If Monica had gone, there was little reason to play along except that Burns still held the deed to the ranch.

Shoving the paper into his jeans, he nodded and walked away without comment. He'd stop by the saloon on his way to the dorm, and if Burns had a problem with that, he could go to hell.

* * *

Monica peered out from behind the fake tree in the hotel hallway again, determined to find out what was going on in room three-twelve. She'd stopped by the saloon and told Mavis where she was going, just in case something happened. Some small portion of her mind admitted that she hoped Harley would track her down too, though it was unlikely he'd be able to get away from her father for the rest of the evening. He'd been so angry, but she couldn't blame him. He'd wanted to help and now his whole life was turned upside down because of her. No wonder he hadn't wanted her take on his family issues. He'd married her, but they weren't family. He was probably afraid she'd screw Betsy's life up too.

The door to three-twelve opened and a tall man stepped out. "Room service should be here any minute. You'll have to eat fast - someone will pick you up at ten for the appointment." Monica couldn't hear the reply, but the man pulled the door closed behind him, and walked down the hall away from her. She took a deep breath in and exhaled slowly as she left her hiding place. She couldn't have asked for a better opportunity, though her hands were already shaking at the thought. Walking quickly toward the elevators, she slipped into a small room to one side just as the staff elevator doors opened.

"Is that for three-twelve?" she asked, relieved to see a glimmer of recognition in the young woman's eyes as she pushed the tray out into the hall.

The woman nodded. "You look familiar - are you new?"

"Sort of. I'm Monica...uh...Majors." The name felt right on her lips. Too right.

The woman's eyes got big. "You're the one that married the boss! Wow. All the girls are so jealous of you..."

Monica smiled, doing her best to look like a happy newlywed, and wondering how the news had spread so quickly. Then again, the compound did seem to run like a small town. "Thank you. I'm really lucky to have him." She paused, her own words reverberating in her head. The guest elevators dinged, reminding her of her mission. "Hey, I was hoping I could deliver this order personally, if you don't mind. Some of my father's friends are visiting, and I wanted to surprise them." She kept smiling, hoping the trembling in her limbs didn't come through in her voice.

"No problem - saves me the work." The woman released her grip on the cart, turning back to the staff elevator. "Just let me know if you need anything else - my name is Christy." Then she was gone, and Monica pushed the cart around the corner and down the hall to the correct door. Squaring her shoulders and schooling her features into what she hoped was a neutral expression, she raised her hand and knocked three times.

"Room service," Monica said loudly, her voice an unwelcome sound in the deserted hallway. A deadbolt snapped open and the door opened a crack, arrested by a short gold chain. A stern man peered out, his eyes moving up and down her body and over the cart as she waited. He closed the door, and she heard the scrape of the chain being removed. He opened the door wide and she pushed the cart in, disconcerted to hear the chain slide back into place and the deadbolt click home.

"This way." The man led the way through an average sized living room to a table in one corner. "You can leave everything here," he said, reaching for one of the plates. She nodded and put all the food on the table, finishing off with a rose in a vase for the center. She wanted to look around, but he watched her constantly, an odd look on his face. When they were finished, she grabbed the cart and walked toward the door, acutely aware of him following. She glanced briefly into a doorway, where a woman sat on a bed next to a child's car seat.

The woman looked up and met Monica's gaze, her eyes widening in recognition. She got off the bed and stood in the doorway, anxiously clasping and unclasping her hands. "What's she doing here?"

"You know her?" The man laid a firm hand on Monica's arm as she tried to continue toward the door. She didn't fight him, hoping that if she went along and acted nonchalant, they'd let her go. After all, she hadn't done anything, really.

The woman frowned. "You don't recognize her? That's Mr. Burns' daughter. I saw a picture of her in his room - is she supposed to be here? Does she know?"

"I know about the package," Monica said, the grip on her arm tightening. "My husband is supposed to deliver it later." A low cry came from behind the woman, and Monica peered into the bedroom, the woman moving to block her view. "How old is your baby?"

The woman laughed. "That's not my kid - I'm just the courier. I'd let you see him, but I wouldn't want you to get attached."

"Courier? But I thought..." Monica felt sick. "The baby - he's the package?"

The guard pulled her away from the bedroom door. "Enough. Irene, see to the child. The driver will be here in ten minutes. I'll call Burns." He pushed Monica onto a couch. "You stay there."

Stunned, Monica nodded. No matter how hard she tried, she couldn't believe that any of this was legitimate - her father just didn't work that way. She tried to process the information, but her mind was spinning out of control. Harley. She needed Harley. Even mad at her, he'd know what to do.

"Yes, sir. I understand." The guard put his cell phone back in his pocket, and motioned for Monica to get up. "You come with me. Your father seems to think you being here will upset your husband and jeopardize our little transaction. So we're going in the bedroom, and you'll stay there until Irene and the kid are gone. Your father will be here shortly to talk to you."

Monica shook her head, staying out of reach as she backed around the couch and tried to figure out how to get past him to the door. "No," she said, her blood racing. "I won't let you do this. It's not right. You can't keep me here." She ran for the door only to be grabbed from behind, her arms pinned to her chest. She kicked and screamed as the man carried her to the bedroom and tossed her on the now-vacant bed. A knee in her back didn't stop her from trying to fight as her wrists and ankles were tied together and a scarf was put in her mouth, tied behind her head. He rolled her over and stood by the bed.

"You'll be more comfortable if you lay on your side," he said, reaching for her shoulder. She shrugged him off, her face hot and tears running down her cheeks. "As soon as Burns gets here, I'll untie you." He turned and walked out of the room, pulling the door shut behind him.

* * *

A baby was crying on the other side of the door when Harley reached room three-twelve. He hesitated before knocking twice. A short, stocky man peered at him through what space the chain would allow, then closed it and slid the metal lock free. The door swung open wide, and a woman carrying a child seat carrier stood just inside the door. She met his gaze with her own icy one. "You're the driver?"

He nodded, frowning as he glanced around the entry. "Where's the package?" Behind the woman on the floor lay a canvas tennis shoe. It reminded him of someone, but who?

"Right here," she said, gesturing to the carrier. "It's none of your concern, you just have to drive us there, and drive me back. You do have the address?"

"Yes." He pushed past the smaller man, slipping by the woman and went to the shoe. Picking it up, he turned it over in his hands. "Who's shoe is this?"

The man strode over and tried to take the item out of Harley's grasp. "It's nothing, just something Lanie dropped." He gestured at the woman then looked pointedly at his watch. "You're going to be late. You need to--"

A loud thump came from behind a closed door down a short hall, followed by a weak whimper that Harley almost didn't hear. Suddenly remembering, he looked inside the back of the shoe to find the faded initials he'd expected. These were the shoes Betsy wore around the ranch when she wasn't working - and she'd loaned them to Monica earlier that morning.

"I'm not going anywhere," he said, walking toward that door. The guard hit him in the stomach, knocking the wind out of him. Harley bent over, and took a right hook to the jaw that caught him off balance. He fell backwards to the floor, kicking a foot out as he went down to connect with the inside of the guard's left knee. The other man went down, and Harley threw himself on top, fastening his hands tightly around that thick neck. He leaned down, so he was eye to eye with the guard as the man fought for air. "That's my wife you have in there, you little prick. You really think anything's going to stop me from getting to her?"

The front door opened, and four hands grabbed Harley, dragging him off the man. "I see I didn't quite make it in time," Mr. Burns said as he approached, his goons holding Harley by each arm. "I hear my daughter is snooping around where she doesn't belong - that's why she's been detained." He smiled, the expression one of indulgent amusement. "Why don't you run along and deliver that package for me, and I'll have her waiting for you when you get back."

"Says the man who tried to marry her off to the highest bidder," Harley said, breathing hard. "I'll just stay here and make sure she's okay. After I do that, we're gonna have a talk about why you want me to deliver a baby to Reno."

* * *

When she heard Harley's voice, Monica frantically tried to think of a way to get his attention. Inching down the bed, she steeled herself for the pain and rolled off the edge, landing on the floor with a thump that jarred every part of her body. She tried to cry out, but only managed a few weak sounds around the cloth in her mouth. Scuffling sounds carried through the floor to her ear, and she hoped - prayed - it was Harley.

Voices rose outside the door, and when she heard "my wife" in that low, raspy timbre, she nearly started to cry again. Blinking back the tears she forced herself to breathe slowly, in and out through her nose. *Don't panic.* Footsteps drew near, and she lifted her head to watch the door. The knob turned, but it was her father who stepped into view.

"Was this really necessary, Jared?" He glanced over his shoulder and the guard slipped into the room, bending down as he flipped open a large pocket knife. Before he could cut her bonds, Harley was by her side, elbowing the other man out of the way. He removed the gag from her mouth then went to work on the rope binding her with the knife Jared had relinquished. Once she was free, he helped her up to sit on the bed and knelt before her, rubbing her wrists with strong, warm fingers.

She looked down into those steel blue eyes, surprised by the depth of emotion reflected back. "Thank you," she whispered, her mouth dry from the gag. Without thinking, she reached out to cup the side of his face, and he leaned into her touch, turning his head slightly to press a kiss to her palm.

"Isn't that just sweet. Don't get too attached, son. She doesn't like to stay in one place."

At her father's voice Monica dropped her hand, the moment broken. She tried to reclaim her other hand, but Harley held it firm in his grasp as he rose to face Burns.

"Oh, I don't know," Harley said thoughtfully. "I think she'd put down roots just fine if she felt safe enough. Now why don't you tell us what's really going on here. I think we have a right to know, since you seem intent on dragging us into it."

Burns nodded. "You're right," he said, turning to his bodyguards standing just inside the door. "Make sure we're not disturbed," he said, watching the door shut behind them. He took a seat in a wicker chair by the closet. "You may as well sit down. This could take awhile."

Harley took a seat on the bed, one arm braced casually behind Monica. She looked at her father, not entirely sure if she wanted his explanation, but needing to know.

"For many years now, I've...arranged for unwanted children to be obtained by people who want them. People who are willing to pay a lot of money for the convenience of not having to deal with government red tape, as well as the shortened time frame. The baby who just left is going to a couple who can't have children, and can't adopt due to some, shall we say, *indiscretions* in the mother's former life."

Monica frowned. "So you just give babies to people who aren't fit to adopt the right way? How do you know those kids will get a good life?"

"We don't," he said with a shrug. "I don't do business with pedophiles, and I have someone drop in on the client for a surprise visit sometime within six months of the transaction. After that, we have no further responsibility. Just like adopting a pet."

Her stomach roiling, Monica shook her head. "How can you say that? You're talking about people's lives - children's futures. How can you just sell them to the highest bidder and move on to the next?" Harley stood, pacing near the end of the bed.

Burns leaned forward, propping his forearms on his knees. "Those kids don't have any chance at all without me. We get them from orphanages, desperate mothers, prisoners, drug addicts. Without me, they'd be turned over to child services and probably forgotten in the system or worse, given to foster parents who just want another government check."

"How long," Monica asked, trying to stay calm. So

many children had visited when she was young, kids she didn't know who stayed a day or two, and then she never saw again. Could this really have been going on all that time?

He sat back in the chair, scrutinizing her carefully. "You were the first."

Chapter Nine

Monica stared at her father. Or was he? "I was the first? But you never sold me..." The meaning behind his words sank in, and what little energy she had drained from her muscles. Harley sat beside her, wrapping an arm around her back to support her. "You bought me," she whispered, nausea tickling her stomach. "You're not my real father. Who am I?"

Harley tried to pull her close, but she pushed him away, anger replacing the shock. She got to her feet, the urge to throw things so strong she thought it might tear her apart. With considerable effort she held steady, her arms shaking as she faced the man who'd made her entire life a lie. "Who. Am. I," she repeated.

Burns rose from the chair. "There's no need for hysterics," he said, flashing a smile that somehow didn't seem sincere. "As far as I'm concerned, you're my daughter. That hasn't changed, and never will."

Monica shook her head, looking at the floor. Her thoughts whirled with the ramifications of what he was telling her. She didn't want to be his daughter, and now as it turned out, she wasn't, not really. But where did she come from? Who was her mother, and how much money had she taken in exchange for her child? The noise in her head grew louder, and suddenly the room was too small. She needed air.

"I have to go," she said, moving quickly toward the door. "I need air." She flung the door open and pushed between the bodyguards standing in her way. Vaguely aware of someone calling her name, she bolted out the apartment door, kicked her remaining shoe off and took the stairs two at a time until she reached the ground floor. Ten more steps and she was outside, striding as fast as she could manage toward the other end of the compound. Five minutes later, she found herself standing in front of Harley's mansion, her chest heaving as she tried to catch her breath and no closer to an answer than she had been. And then she felt it, sharper than it had ever been before.

It was time to leave.

She jogged up the stairs and through the house, waiting impatiently for the elevator to take her down to the basement. She'd use the tunnel Betsy had shown her, and escape into the night. She only hoped her father - *Mr. Burns* - would go easy on Harley after she left.

The corridor was darker than she remembered, and her heart raced, every sound sending another jolt of awareness through her system. Cold seeped through her socks and she swore under her breath, hesitating only a moment to consider going back for shoes. Panic drove her on. Just before she reached the door to the tunnel, her senses went on high alert, and she stopped, peering cautiously down into the near-darkness. "Is someone there?"

A male figure detached from the black wall, moving slowly toward her and blocking her way out. "Just me," Harley said, stopping to look down at her with such concern it brought the tears she'd been fighting to the fore. "I had a feeling you might decide to run. I was hoping I might be able to change your mind." He reached out to touch the side of her face and she batted his hand away. He stepped closer, repeating the gesture. The look on his face was so caring that she allowed it. She didn't want to feel alone anymore, and somehow she knew he'd stay beside her, no matter what.

The tears fell finally, sobs wracking her body as she leaned into his broad chest. His arms curved around her, holding her tight as he pressed a kiss to her temple. Then he was lifting her, carrying her down the hall. She clung to him as he set her gently in the middle of his bed and laid down beside her, pulling a blanket up to cover them both.

As her sobs subsided, Monica loosened her grip on Harley's shirt, resting her fingers against his chest. His heart beat a slow, steady rhythm under her hand and she snuggled closer, her face against the side of his neck. He stroked a hand over her arm and pressed his lips to her forehead before skimming his knuckles lightly across the side of her breast. She looked up into his eyes. The mixture of concern and desire she saw there nearly brought her to tears again.

"Thank you," she whispered. "I don't want to leave, Harley. I want to stay here - with you."

He nodded, leaning close so that his lips were just a breath away from hers. "Then stay," he said, his tongue flicking out just to tease at the corner of her mouth. "Everything will work out. I promise." His mouth closed over hers and she sighed, closing her eyes. His kiss pushed all the bad feelings to the recesses of her mind, and she pulled him closer, hungrily taking everything he offered.

He broke the kiss slowly, nipping and licking at her lips before he used his hands to tilt her head up. He ran his tongue down the center of her throat to lave the hollow at the base. Monica arched up, her body begging for more and he gave it to her, stopping only to draw her shirt over her head, then trailing kisses down the center of her chest and between her breasts. He traced one nipple through her bra with the tip of his finger and she arched up again. "Please, Harley."

He chuckled low in his throat, the sound sending

chills of pleasure right down to her core as he pulled the thin fabric aside and sucked the sensitive tip into his mouth. She whimpered, unable to remain still as his other hand slipped between her legs and lightly scraped a blunt fingernail over the front of her jeans. Her hips bucked, and he palmed her breast with one hand as he moved lower, kissing her ribs, her stomach, and exploring her navel with her tongue. She writhed in pleasure, her whole body on fire even as he removed her jeans. Raising her head at the fluttering touch she felt at her ankle, she opened her eyes and looked at her feet to see him kissing his way up her leg, his strong hands kneading the muscles as he went. It was wickedly delicious, and he looked up to meet her eyes. "You are gorgeous, darlin'," he said, his gaze never wavering from hers. He continued up her leg, kissing and kneading until he reached the juncture of her thigh. She watched as he licked his lips, then slowly began to circle the sensitive spot between her legs, flicking her clit and driving her into a frenzy. Her head fell back and she closed her eyes as he took her higher, the heat at her center building with every lick and swirl of his tongue.

Her release came swiftly, her entire body shivering as the shocks rippled under her skin as her head whirled. Harley came up beside her, folding her in his arms and holding her tight from behind until the waves of pleasure subsided. Words to tell him how she felt, what he meant to her drifted through her mind, but she remained silent as he pulled the blanket up over them again. She tried to turn, wanted to give him what he'd given her, but he held her still.

"Shh..." he breathed in her ear, stroking her hair back with one hand. "We'll figure all this out tomorrow. Sleep."

* * *

The sound of running water woke Monica the next morning. She stretched her arms overhead and glanced at the partially shut door to the master bathroom. An image of Harley in the shower came to mind, warm water sluicing down his sculpted, naked body as he tilted his head back, running his hands though that long sandy hair. A shiver went through her as she remembered the night before, the horrible news and how Harley had been waiting for her. He'd broken the cycle, stopped her from running. Made it okay to stay.

He'd saved her. Again.

She tossed the covers back and crawled out of bed, pushing back the nagging guilt that she should be more upset about what she'd learned last night. Instead she felt lighter, as if she'd just been released from a dark prison cell. She wasn't Burns' daughter. He had no claim on her.

But the man in the shower did. The man who'd risked everything to help her, even before he really knew her. The man who still hadn't given up on her, even when she was ready to give up on everything. Her heart racing, she pushed the bathroom door open and slipped inside, the damp heat enveloping her as she stood staring at the opaque white curtain. She wanted to go to him, but a tiny niggle of doubt held her in place.

"You just gonna stand there all day, or you wanna come scrub my back?"

The teasing comment washed away the last of her fear, as he grinned at her around the curtain. "I might even wash yours if you're lucky." She smiled and stepped into the shower. He wrapped his arms around her and bent down for a kiss so tender and...*loving* she nearly forgot to breath. "Better this morning?" he asked, guiding her under the spray. She nodded and closed her eyes as he gently tipped her head back, his fingers smoothing the water into her hair. Bliss.

Then his lips were on the side of her neck, licking, sucking, and moving lower. She sighed, her arms sliding over his shoulders as he took the peak of one nipple between his lips. She arched into him, only his hands at her hips keeping her from falling back as he pulled and nipped at her breast. Heat and moisture between her legs brought a moan to her lips, and she grasped his head, pulling him up to meet her eyes.

"Inside me," she said, her voice raspy with need. "Now, please."

Harley nodded. "Yes ma'am." He lifted her up and she wrapped her legs around his waist, sinking down onto his thick, rigid cock with a whimper of delight. He turned to brace her against the wall, and then took her lips, his tongue plundering her mouth as he thrust in and out, in and out in a slow, steady rhythm.

He pulled back an inch, and she opened her eyes to find him staring at her with an intensity that blew her away. "You're mine," he growled, punctuating the statement with a hard thrust. "You'll always be mine. Don't ever leave."

Tears threatened as she shook her head. "I'm yours," she said, leaning forward to kiss him softly as she tightened her inner muscles around him. "I won't leave. Ever. I love you."

He pressed his lips to hers again and buried his face in her neck as he pounded into her against the shower wall, as if desperate to mark his claim. Her eyes fluttered closed as the tension built between her legs, her whole body spasming as she came, wave after wave of pure bliss radiating over and through her skin. He lifted her higher, his shaft sliding free and she whimpered again as he lowered her to her feet, holding her tight against him as she rode out the orgasm.

When she could breathe again, she looked up at him, caressing his jaw with her hand. "You didn't..."

He shrugged, his lips turned up slightly. "No con-dom." He turned off the cooling water and pushed the shower curtain aside. Stepping out of the bathtub, he reached for a towel, but Monica grabbed his arm.

"Not so fast, mister." she grinned, stepping out next to him and sitting on the edge of the tub. Grasping his hips, she leaned forward, flicking the end of his cock with her tongue. With a wink, she took him into her mouth, her gaze locked on his as she sucked him deeper. He groaned, his fingers running through her hair as she pulled back slowly then pushed forward again. She licked and swirled her tongue, working him with her mouth until he began thrusting his hips forward, gentle but insistent. Circling the fingers of one hand around the base of his shaft, she pulled and pumped and sucked until his body stiffened, the warmth of his release flowing down her throat.

"Wow." Harley took a deep breath, letting it out slowly. He helped Monica to her feet, nearly stumbling backward into the counter as his own equilibrium malfunctioned. Wrapping his arms around her, he held tight, part of him daring to hope that she meant what she'd said. The other part warning him to wait and see. Reluctantly he loosened his hold and grabbed the towel he'd been reaching for earlier. He tossed it around her shoulders, stifling the urge to rub her down himself. "We'd better get moving," he said, his tone harsher than he'd intended judging by the question in Monica's eyes. He winked as he wrapped a towel around his own waist. "I really don't think we're going to get anything done until we put some clothes on...unless you'd rather not. I'm sure we could find some way to keep ourselves entertained for the day..."

She giggled. "Go get dressed," she said, playfully tossing her towel at him. "I'll just brush my teeth and meet you in the kitchen...say, twenty minutes?"

He nodded, just happy to see her smiling as he turned and walked out of the room. She probably wouldn't be by the time they were done talking. They needed to figure out how to get evidence against her father, something that would ensure that he'd be locked up for life. If the FBI agent posing as a body-guard couldn't get anything, he had little hope they'd be able to. Still, he had to try. Not just for the ranch, but for her as well. Monica had been put through the wringer by Burns, and that was enough to put him away for good, from Harley's perspective.

He pulled on clean jeans and a tight black t-shirt, then padded out to the kitchen in bare feet. He put a pot of coffee on and set the counter island with two bowls, spoons, glasses, and a box of cereal. He was just getting the milk out of the fridge when Monica joined him.

"Better?" she asked with a grin, scooting onto a padded bar stool.

He stood back, pretending to study her like an artist sizing up a subject. "No." He shook his head in mock disappointment. "But it will do for awhile, I guess." He joined her, putting the milk between them on the counter. "Help yourself," he said, trying to de-

cide how to approach the conversation they needed
to have. He decided to start with the truth.

"There's an FBI agent working undercover for
Burns, but he hasn't been able to get anything because Burns keeps the business so far removed from
himself most of the time. This is the first chance he's
had to even get close, but he asked for my help. If I—
we, can get him something, he'll be able to pass it
back to the proper authorities."

She poured milk on her cereal and handed the con-
tainer to him. "Well, we should start by talking to him
then," she said, her gaze focused on her bowl. "I
don't know what kind of evidence he needs, but we
should get it fast before my...uh, Burns decides to
split." She glanced at him, her expression neutral.

Harley nodded. It was probably for the best, this
cool detachment, considering what her role would
have to be for the duration. Still, he rubbed a hand
over her shoulder, pleased when a hint of warmth
tinged her cheeks at his touch. "You're going to have
to convince Burns that you forgive him," he said, feeling her shiver under his fingers. "Not just to get evidence, but to stay safe. If he thinks you might go to the
police, there's no telling what he'll do to keep that
from happening. If anything happened to you..."

She leaned toward him, resting her head against his
chest as he hugged her close. "I've been pretending to
be his daughter for nearly as long as I've been alive,"
she said, kissing his jaw before pushing gently out of

his embrace. "I'll manage until we can throw the bastard in jail."

Harley grinned. "That's my girl." He took his cell
phone out of his pocket and dialed Burns' number.
"Might as well get this ball rolling," he said, holding
the phone to his ear.

Chapter Ten

Monica bent low over the green felt, cradling the stick between her thumb and forefinger as she lined up a shot on the eight ball. It was a perfect, straight shot into the corner pocket and under normal circumstances she'd make it every time. Pivoting the stick just a tiny bit on her hand, she drew back and popped the cue ball, striking the eight enough off-center to send it careening recklessly into the rail and back down toward the other end of the table.

"Oops!" she said, giggling as she stood and backed away, stumbling over her own feet just enough to make it believable. "Don't know how I mished that," she slurred at a grinning Harley. His smile was genuine, and she thought maybe he was enjoying her role just a little too much. Would he help her line up the next shot, she wondered?

"I think maybe you've had too much to drink,

sweetheart." He came in close, bracing one hand on her back for support as he leaned in to kiss her neck. "Ready?" he whispered in her ear before straightening to look at her. She nodded, trying to ignore her body's reaction to him as she spun around to fall neatly against the high table Burns and his bodyguards were sitting at. Glasses went flying despite the best efforts of the guards, and Monica stifled a laugh at the look on Burns' face when his Jack and water ended up in his lap.

"I'm shor--sorry," she said, real laughter on her lips. "I think I'm a little...tipsy." She leaned to the side, stumbling against the nearest bodyguard who caught her arms and set her upright. "I think maybe I should go home." She stepped back, tripping over her heel and falling against Harley's chest. Just where she wanted to be. Too bad she couldn't stay.

He chuckled low in her ear. "Well done, honey." Then he raised his head to peer over her shoulder. "Would you mind if Monica borrowed one of your bodyguards to take her back to our place? I've got some things to finish up, and I don't think she should be wandering around in her condition, if you know what I mean."

Burns shook his head, disapproval in his gaze as he watched Monica. She avoided eye contact, kept looking everywhere but at him as though she couldn't focus on anything. Finally he shrugged, gesturing to the nearest bodyguard. "Escort Ms. Burns home, then come right back here."

"Majors," Monica corrected, surprised when the name rolled off her lips. "I'm married now, Daddy, don't you remember?" She raised her left hand, wiggling her ring at him with an exaggerated motion. Somehow she managed not to let her middle finger float out at him.

"Alright darlin'." Harley grasped her shoulders and turned her to face a tall, broad-shouldered man. "It's time to go. This nice man is going to see you home safely, and I'll be along in an hour or so. Don't give him any trouble, okay?"

"Mmm...K," she purred, stepping forward to place both hands on the man's chest. "I'm sure we'll get along just fine." She grinned, then took his hand and started pulling him towards the door. She remembered to bump against tables, chairs and people on her way out for effect, tugging the bodyguard out onto the old-looking wooden porch and down the stairs of the Double D. They walked down the center of the road, passing a group of harem girls all scurrying quickly in the opposite direction. After they'd gone, Monica turned to her would-be protector.

"What's your name?" she said, pitching her voice high and valley-girl. He merely smiled and kept walking. Okay then, she thought. "Because my husband Harley said your name was Daniels. He said you might talk to me like you talked to him that one night."

She wondered if she'd made a mistake when the bodyguard just kept walking, ignoring her question. Maybe this wasn't the undercover agent after all, though Harley had seemed certain. Perhaps she'd just played her part too well. But if this wasn't the guy, she couldn't afford to have him running back to her father with the news that he was being set up. She decided to try a different approach. It was risky, but they were almost to the mansion and she was running out of time.

"So, Mr. Tough Guy..." she weaved a little, bumping him with her shoulder. "Hypothetically speaking, what's the biggest thing my dad has to watch out for so he doesn't get caught doing...well, you know. What he does."

He glanced at her, his eyes calculating. She met his gaze straight on, hoping he wouldn't think she was trying to trap him. Or if he did, that he'd play along anyway to prove his loyalty.

"Your husband told you to ask me that?"

They'd reached the front steps of the mansion, and she led him inside. She didn't answer until they were safely in the elevator going down. Deciding to play her hand and risk it all, she turned to face the bodyguard.

"He said you were undercover," she finally replied, dropping all pretense of intoxication. "We know he's smuggling children, babies mostly. What we don't know is what you need to lock him away for life."

Thick tension filled the small space as he stared at her with narrowed eyes, and for a long moment she thought she'd made a colossal mistake. The elevator doors opened, and she moved to exit, but he stepped around her to block her path. Her heart pounded as she backed away, stopping only when her shoulders pressed into the far wall of the car.

"Why would you set your own father up," he asked, dropping one hand to into the opposite side of his suit jacket.

Monica swallowed hard. "He's not my father," she said, noting surprise on the man's face. "According to what he told me last night, I was his first...purchase."

The hand she'd assumed was reaching for a gun re-appeared with a cell phone instead. She let out the breath she'd been holding, relieved that she wasn't going to be shot. At least for now. He dialed a number, his eyes glancing from her to the floor and back again as he waited.

"Mr. Burns?"

Monica felt her stomach drop as he spoke. Oh God. Harley was still at the bar. What would they do to him for her disloyalty?

"This is Daniels. Your daughter is safe at home. I'll be back shortly." He nodded, then disconnected the call, stowing the phone back in his pocket. He gestured her Monica to follow him. "That will buy us a few minutes. Show me where you live."

Monica nodded, fear and anger battling in her

head. She led the way down the hall and unlocked the door to the suite, then locked it behind them. "Please, just tell me," she said as she turned to face him. "Whatever you need, we'll get. Anything to put him behind bars for good." *And out of my life.*

"You're sure it's babies he's selling?"

Monica nodded, her arms crossed over her chest. "The one I saw was a baby - pretty young too. Though he implied that I was bought as a child."

Daniels stared at the floor for a long moment before looking back up at her. "I'll need a sample of your hair, for starters. And something to wrap it in. It's a long shot, but your biological parents may have regretted their decision and put a missing persons report out. We'll see."

She took a step back, wary. "I don't want to find my real parents..."

"You don't ever have to know who they are or talk to them if you don't want, but it would be a solid foundation for the case if they came forward. Plus we can prove you're not Burns' daughter by comparing your DNA to his." He waited patiently, his expression clearly expecting her eventual cooperation. So like Harley, she thought, though not nearly as potent.

"Fine." She sighed. "What else?"

He glanced at his watch. "Any kind of pictures or video would be the best evidence. DNA from the kids would be handy too, along with any paperwork at all you can find. Really anything you can find that links your...Burns to the activity will be helpful. There's no such thing as too much."

She nodded. "Okay. We can do that." She reached up and yanked a few hairs from low on her head, and put them into a small envelope that was lying on the hall table. "How do we let you know when we have something?"

He took the envelope and slipped it in the inner pocket of his jacket. "Have Harley text me from his phone with 'all clear'. I can explain that easily enough if Burns asks and I'll get in touch with him on his phone as soon as I can get away." He took a pen and small notepad out of his pocket to write on, then handed her a slip of paper with the number. "I've got to get back, but thank you. If you two can get me enough evidence, we can put Burns away for a long, long time. I'll do what I can to help now that I know what's going on." He gave her the briefest smile and let himself out, shutting the door tight behind him.

Monica snapped the deadbolt in place, suddenly feeling very exposed. What if Daniels wasn't really an agent? Or what if he was, and her father found out before they could get any evidence? She rubbed the back of her neck, closing her eyes and wishing Harley was there. He'd hold her, kiss her, tell her everything would be all right. Her lips curved up in a smile just thinking of his warm touch, and as if on cue, a key rattled in the lock, popping the deadbolt open.

She turned to meet him, hugging herself as the

door opened to keep from throwing herself into his arms. It took a moment for her to process that the man in the doorway wasn't Harley.

"What are you doing here? And how did you get a key?"

"Oh come now, Monica. Is that any way to greet your father?" Stephen Burns stepped into the apartment, his arms stretched wide. He smirked at her and lowered his arms as Daniels and Harley entered, followed by two men she'd never seen before. "I've enjoyed this little game of cat and mouse, but I'm afraid that finding out both my bodyguard and my daughter are disloyal has put me in somewhat of a foul mood."

"But how--" Monica stopped, her blood pressure rising. He had been listening the whole time. All the years she'd spent living with this man - running from him, and she hadn't thought to worry about listening devices. She bit her bottom lip, shaking her head slowly. "You've been listening all along, haven't you? When did you plant the bug?"

He laughed, the sound bouncing too loudly around the small room. "I have your husband and your FBI agent waiting for me to decide their fate and you want to know when I planted the bug? No wonder I finally caught you. You have your priorities all wrong, darling."

"On the contrary, *Mr. Burns*. For once in my life, I have my priorities right where they should be." She met Harley's gaze, saw the corner of his lips just barely turn up before she focused on Burns again. "Since you brought it up though, what are you going to do with us? Assuming you aren't going to just make us disappear, that is. People might notice if the owner of the compound goes missing...not to mention a federal agent."

"I'm hurt that you think I could do that to my own daughter." Burns smacked his left palm to his chest in a dramatic mocking gesture. "And since you're married, your husband is family. I might get mad at him once in a while, but as long as he doesn't hurt you, he's welcome with us."

Monica wanted to take comfort in the words, but she still nibbled her lower lip. "And Agent Daniels?"

Burns lowered his gaze to the floor. "An undercover snitch is another matter, I'm afraid." He looked up, his eyes hard and glittering. Monica glanced at Daniels, noting the weary, resigned look on his face. It occurred to her that once again, she'd put a man in danger just by being who she was. She looked at Burns, who met her gaze and held it. "Snitches are a liability, and if I allow one to live, loyalty will be much harder to come by in staff. No, I need to make an example, so others know there are consequences to their actions." He nodded to the man behind Daniels, who cocked his gun, the sound ringing just as loud as any shot.

"Wait!" Monica stepped forward, unable to just watch the man get shot. "There has to be some other way - can't you just send him off somewhere and say he disappeared or was murdered or whatever?"

Burns shook his head. "Sorry. There's only one outcome to this." He motioned to the door. "Not in front of the kids, Steve." The man prodded the small of Daniels' back with his gun, and Daniels didn't look back as he walked to the door. Monica swiped at a tear, taking a step toward Harley before she realized what she was doing.

"You're a beast, and I'm glad I'm not related to you," she said, blinking her eyes quickly. A muffled shot in the hall made her gasp, and she finally ran to Harley, not caring what happened. He folded her in his arms, his embrace calming her nerves even though the danger was still very real.

"Very touching," Burns said, his tone mocking. "Andrew, please make the lovebirds comfortable in the master suite. They'll be more comfortable there while I'm processing the last of the merchandise."

Chapter Eleven

Burns' goon gestured toward the hall with his gun and Harley kept one arm around Monica's shoulders as they walked to the master suite. Anger and guilt settled like lead in his gut as the door to the bedroom shut firmly behind them. He should have known about the bugs, should have never let her go through with this scheme. She'd been insistent about her role though and he'd finally given in against his better judgment.

He caressed the side of her face with one hand, the other pulling her in towards his chest. She offered no resistance as he tilted her chin up and kissed her once, softly. Leaning forward, he embraced her, his lips just a hair away from her ear.

"I'm sorry," he whispered, careful to keep his voice as low as possible. "It's going to be okay, but I need your help now if we're going to get out of here. Are you up to it?"

Monica nodded almost imperceptibly. He rubbed her back with slow circles that he hoped would ease some of the tension emanating off her in waves. "Let's take a shower," he said, making no effort to hide his voice. She nodded and stood, swiping at the damp area under her eyes with her fingers.

"Okay," she said, holding her hand out to him. The gesture of trust wasn't lost on him, and he brought her fingers to his lips before leading her toward the bathroom. Closing the door behind them, he winked at her, turned on the water in the sink and then leaned in to start the shower, turning the tap on full blast. When he turned back, she was just reaching for the hem of her shirt, but he shook his head.

"The shower will have to wait, if that's okay," he said just above a whisper. "I just needed some background noise so we can get out of here."

She frowned, glancing around the smallish room. "I don't see any windows..."

He chuckled. "There aren't any down here. But I have something better." He grabbed her hand and reached for the light switch, plunging the room into total darkness, just in case Burns had planted cameras too, the sick bastard. "Don't let go of my hand," he said, tugging Monica along as he made his way across the room to a small linen closet. He pulled the door open and reached in, running his free hand over the back wall about six feet up. Finally feeling the latch, he pushed it, and a slight click signaled his success. He turned to the right and stepped forward, pushing against the side wall. It swung away from him and he stepped into the old tunnel, making sure Monica was clear of the door before closing it firmly behind them.

"Where are we?" Monica's grip tightened on his hand, and he squeezed back to reassure her, his foot sweeping wide along the dirt floor. Something solid impeded his movement and he bent down to retrieve the heavy-duty flashlight he'd been looking for. Switching it on, he turned the beam enough to let him see Monica's surprised expression. "Another tunnel?"

He nodded, grabbing her hand again and pulling her down the dark shaft. "There are several of them beneath the compound, many of them connecting to various buildings and underground meeting rooms. Betsy and I discovered them by accident when we bought the place - as near as we can tell, this must have been home to some sort of cult or secretive group at some point." He took a right down another tunnel, stopping at an old wooden door. "This is one of the rooms we're renovating for the harem fantasy - there's a stairwell inside that goes up to Sultan's Castle. We should be safe here until we figure out what to do about your father - the room isn't available to guests yet."

He led her inside and reached out to pull an ornate red tassel that hung from the ceiling. Lavender light bathed the room in a mellow haze.

"Wow," she breathed, wonder and appreciation on her face. "This is amazing."

* * *

Harley watched Monica take it all in, his eyes never leaving her face as she took in the nearly-finished harem suite. The fear he'd seen just a short while ago was gone, appreciative wonder lighting her face.

"You're amazing," he said, moving behind her and sliding his hands over his hips and around her waist, cocooning her in his embrace. She didn't move away, putting her hands lightly over his. Her touch sent blood rushing straight between his thighs, and he bent his head low, pressing a gentle kiss to her neck before straightening again.

He glanced over her head at the walls, the dirt hidden by a stone veneer covering and topped with yards and yards of wispy, light blue tulle. In the center of the matching tiled floor there was a sunken area with benches around the edge covered in large, ornate pillows. In the middle on a huge blue Persian rug, a huge round bed sat dressed in a pastel yellow satin comforter with more pillows stacked up against a curved brass headboard. A gleaming gold halo supported by four posters held a curtain of filmy blue and white silks, hung at different heights for a seductive, inviting look.

Monica slowly let her head fall back to rest against

his chest. "It's already perfect - what's left?" She turned her head, looking up at him with wide, soft eyes. He bent down to place a soft kiss on her moist lips, his erection pressing against her ass.

"It needs girls," he said, grinning when she rolled her eyes and turned away, though she seemed content to stay in his arms. "These are fantasy suites, darlin'. We make money giving people what they want. And some people fantasize about being in or having a harem."

She turned in his arms, her hands on his chest. "Do you fantasize about having a harem?" A wink told him she was teasing, and he laughed, his knuckles gently rubbing the sides of her ribcage. Something like hope swelled inside him.

"Nah." He chuckled, tweaking her pebbled nipples through her shirt. "One woman's enough trouble for me," he said with a smirk.

Those delectable lips pursed in mock offense, and she pushed hard against his chest, the unexpected move sending him back a couple of steps. She turned and walked away, down the steps into the sunken area. "You're going to pay for that, Harlan Majors."

He grinned, noting she was headed in the general direction of that big bed. Jogging to catch up, he grabbed her by the waist just as she reached out to touch one of the bits of hanging silk. "Bring it on, sweetheart," he murmured in her ear as she pretended to struggle. "Let's see what you've got." He tossed her

on the bed, earning a shriek of surprise for the effort.
Settling between her legs he braced himself on his elbows and looked down into her sparkling eyes. "You
were saying something about payment?"

"Was I?" Her voice was husky, and his smile faded
as a contemplative look crossed her face. "I seem to
have forgotten..."

He captured her lips with his own then, his tongue
dancing with hers as he moved his hips against her
pelvis. She moaned low in her throat, wrapping her
arms around his neck and pulling him tight against
her. He needed no further encouragement - even if
she didn't stay, they both needed this, needed each
other.

In no mood to be patient, he pulled back, yanking
his shirt over his head. "I want you naked in twenty
seconds," he said, reaching for the button on his
jeans. He shimmied out of them and looked over at
Monica, her elbows propped up on the bed and an
appreciative look in her eye.

"When did you get so bossy?" she asked, sitting up
and pulling her shirt off. Harley tried to think of a
witty come back as he watched, but words deserted
him as soon as he saw those gorgeous breasts. She
smiled, knowingly. "A little distracted, Majors?"

Harlan nodded, stepping forward to reach for the
button on her pants. "I suspect that's the way you
want it, witch." He pulled her jeans off her hips, and
tossed them aside then pushed her legs apart. "So

pink," he said, caressing her inner lips with one finger. "So pretty." He knelt between her legs and trailed kisses up the inside of her thigh to her warm, wet core. Swirling and licking, he played between her legs, pumping two fingers in and out of her sheath as he flicked at her clit. Monica arched up, moaning and he moved over her, sucking one small earlobe into his mouth as he buried his pulsing cock in her warmth.

Monica cried out as Harley pushed inside her. It was too much and not enough all at once, and she moved her hips against him as he thrust in and out sending currents of pleasure up her spine. His tongued kisses on her neck completed the circuit, her entire body a relentless mass of swirling energy. Harder and faster, she met him again and again as he brought her to the edge, reaching between them to press a finger against her center at the same time his teeth closed over the spot where her neck and shoulder joined. As she shattered around him, felt his warm seed spilling deep within her, she realized that this time he was claiming her. Marking her as his in a primal, instinctual way.

She should mind. She should push him away; ask him just what the hell he thought he was doing not using a condom.

She didn't.

He lay spent on top of her, his arms curled protectively under her shoulders and his face still resting against her neck. She caressed his shoulders and back with her fingertips, laying slow, gentle kisses across the top of his shoulder. He moved, bracing himself on his elbows as he raised his head to look in her eyes.

"Stay with me, sweetheart. Not just until Burns is gone, but after that. Promise me." His gaze was so intense, possessive and unapologetic. From any other man, it would be intimidating, but she'd known him long enough to understand it for what it was. Reassurance that he wanted her. That he would take care of her. Somehow he seemed to know exactly what she needed, and she was grateful.

She smoothed one hand over the side of his face, blinking back tears. "I'll stay," she whispered, her throat too tight for anything more. "I promise."

Harley nodded, leaning in to place a soft, moist kiss on her lips. Then he moved off of her and she shuddered as the cold air hit her vulnerable skin. Emotions raw, she sat up in a daze and reached for her shirt.

"Hey." She turned to look at the man responsible for her emotional state. He smiled, brushing a few stray hairs out of her face. "You okay?"

She nodded; forcing what she hoped was a reassuring smile. "Sure. Absolutely." Closing her eyes she accepted another kiss, and then allowed him to pull her to her feet. "So now what?" she said, mentally trying to shake off both the fog in her head and the residual feelings of doubt and fear that threatened to surface again.

He shrugged, turning to pull his own shirt on. "Now we get that evidence against Burns and nail his ass."

Monica finished buttoning her jeans. "Good plan. Any ideas on how we do that, now that Daniels is...uh, gone, and we aren't exactly on the inside anymore?"

"I've been giving that a lot of thought, actually." He took her hand and brought it to his lips, pressing a cavalier kiss on her fingers. "Honey, I think it's time to buy a baby."

Monica smiled indulgently. "That's great," she said, slipping her fingers out of Harley's grasp. "But I think you're forgetting that everyone knows what we look like. Wouldn't it be better if we had someone else do it? Like the police?"

He shrugged. "Do you really want to take the chance that Burns has the local police in his pocket? I think it would be safer to get the information and go straight to the FBI with it. All we have to do is set up the meet, tape the whole thing, and get ourselves and the evidence to the FBI."

"You make it sound so easy - but you still haven't told me how we're going to get around the fact that they've all seen us."

He grinned, reaching out to run a hand along a pile of beaded silk on the table behind him. "We specialize in fantasies here, sweetheart. When we get done,

Burns won't recognize either one of us."

Monica followed him up a steep spiral staircase in the corner. He pushed open the red door at the top and they entered a huge, cavernous room with another sunken circle in the center. Ornate chaise lounges and more of the large silky pillows were scattered everywhere, and there appeared to be about a couple dozen girls in scant harem attire doting on just three men in flowing robes, each commanding his own lounger.

She followed Harley to the imposing double doors at the far end of the room and out of the harem, into a wide hall with shiny stone floors and thick white columns. Big potted plants gave it a lush feel, and small raised islands filled with fine white sand reminded her of a desert oasis. "So the room below is for..."

"Couples or groups who want a slightly more private fantasy." Harley winked, and then pulled her past the front doors and down a side hall, staying away from the generous windows that fronted the main road on the ranch. "There's someone I want you to meet. You can stay with her while I go gather a few things we'll need. I'll have her bring you to the salon when we're ready."

She tried to pull out of his grip, but he held tight. "Wait. Why can't I go with you? And what are you going to get? Let me go!" She yanked hard and her feet slipped on the smooth floor as her hand came free. Landing on her butt, she slid backwards into a stone column, her head knocking against the surface with a resounding thud.

Harley was kneeling in front of her in two seconds, his worried eyes looking down into hers as he cradled her head in his hands. "Monica? Honey? Talk to me, sweetheart. I need to know you're okay..."

She winced at how loud the words sounded. "You don't have to shout. Ow..." Lifting a hand to the back of her head, she felt around for the bruised spot as he lifted her to her feet. "Damn that...whoa..." she swayed, a touch of dizziness pulling her off balance.

"Easy there." Harley pulled her close and kissed her forehead, then leaned down and picked her up in his arms. "We need to get some ice, and I'll have the doctor come take a look. You're gonna have a nasty bump, if nothing else."

Closing her eyes, she rested her head against his shoulder, her head throbbing too much to argue. "I'm sorry," she murmured, opening her eyes to look up at him as he carried her down the hall. "I didn't mean--"

"Shh." He stopped in front of a door and bent his head to place a soft kiss on her lips. "It wasn't your fault - I'm the one who needs to apologize." Without taking his gaze from hers, he kicked on the door three times. "I want you to be safe. Please wait for me here?"

Monica nodded, wincing at the motion as the door opened. She glanced over to see a tall, willowy blond

with straight hair and an abundance of eyeliner looking at them with an amused expression.

"Monica Majors, meet Veronica Rowan."

Chapter Twelve

Monica did her best to smile as Harley carried her into Veronica's dressing room. He finally put her down, keeping his hands at her waist to steady her.

"Geez Harley. I know you want to set up a caveman fantasy, but I'm not sure getting clubbed on the head is gonna trigger that 'take me like an animal' instinct, if you know what I mean."

Monica turned around to look at the blond. Veronica winked, her lips curved up in an impish smile. Monica grinned back.

"I--that's not what happened," he stuttered.

"A club-shaped pillow might work better," Monica quipped, earning a squeeze at her waist where Harley still supported her. "But sadly, I can't let him take credit for this. I slipped on the floor in the hall and slid into one of those gorgeous columns." She reached to feel the back of her head. "How could you tell? I didn't think it was that--" Warm, sticky fluid coated her fingers, and she looked at them in shock. " Oh. I'm...uh...bleeding."

Veronica took her hand. "Come with me, and we'll get you cleaned up. It's probably not as bad as it seems - head wounds bleed a lot." She pulled her past a rack of clothing and a cluttered makeup table to a small bathroom, patting the side of the bathtub. "Sit here and I'll get a towel and some ice." Harley stood in the doorway, holding his phone to one ear.

"I need you at the harem right away. Room 104....that's right, Veronica's room. It's not her though, and I'd rather you kept this between us." He paused, glancing over at Monica quickly before turning away. "A head injury, but she's conscious." He finished the call and tucked his phone in his pocket. "I've got to go...but I'll be back as soon as I can."

Monica nodded as something cold pressed against the back of her head. "Be careful," she said, reaching up to hold the ice pack in place. He nodded and walked away without so much as a backward look. After the door shut, Veronica came around to lean against the vanity, arms crossed over her chest.

"Okay, spill. What the heck's going on here? I can't believe he would do something like this, but if he hurt you..."

Monica shook her head, the movement making her head spin. "No! He'd never hurt me." She waited until the room stopped moving and considered how much she should say, knowing from the look on Veronica's face that she wasn't going to buy some lame story. Still, it would be better not to share details. Not yet, anyway. "I sort of got Harley in some trouble," she said carefully. "Big trouble. And we're trying to fix it."

Veronica stared at her, her brow creased in thought. Someone knocked at the door, and she finally nodded. "I'm a personal security trainer when I'm not working here," she said, her tone the same as if she'd been talking about the weather. "Before you leave, I'll show you some moves that might come in handy."

* * *

Harley dialed another number as he made his way to the back of the building. On the fourth ring, a groggy voice answered.

"Alex? Sorry to wake you, but I need a favor. My wife and I need to change our appearance for a while, something conservative, but rich. Think you can handle that?" He heard fabric rustling on the other end, and then paper rattling.

"You got married? How did that happen?" The makeup artist sounded unimpressed, not that Harley could blame him. Two days ago he wouldn't have believed it himself.

"It's not important - I can explain later. I'm surprised you hadn't heard already. Everyone else seems to know."

Alex chuckled on the other end of the line. "I took a few days off, and the girls aren't here yet. Wanna bet who will rush to tell me first?"

Harley grinned. "Nope. I just hope no one gets hurt in that race. Can you have that stuff ready for us later this morning? We've kind of got a situation to deal with."

"Sure. I'll get going on it right away. Wanna meet me in the studio anytime after six?"

Harley nodded, checking his watch. Two hours should be enough time to collect what he needed from security and get back to Monica. "Yep - can do. Thanks Alex, I owe you one."

The other man laughed. "Buy me a beer this week-end, and we'll call it good."

"Deal." Harley put the phone back in his pocket, and slipped out the back door. Hopefully daybreak was still an hour off - the darkness would provide good cover for moving around the compound. The surveillance equipment would be hard enough to get with Burns' security detail right there, but he also needed to break into the suite Burns was working out of, and steal a buyer's name so they could intercept the hand-off. It was too late to set up a real transaction, but posing as clients should do the trick. He didn't want to drag this out. It ended today.

Moving quickly and staying in the shadows, he circled wide to approach the dormitory from behind.

A single sentry stood by the back door, the orange glow of a cigarette marking his position. Harley decided the direct approach was probably the easiest, and strode boldly out into the empty yard.

Dropping his cigarette, the guard came away from the wall to meet him. "Who are yo--"

Without hesitation, Harley put his fist into the man's face, watching with satisfaction as the guard spun around to land face-first on the ground. Harley bent over to make sure the man was out cold, then stepped over him and let himself into the building. Taking the stairs two at a time, he reached the third floor quickly, knowing he didn't have much time until the guard came to outside. He reached into his pocket for keys as he walked toward room 312, stopping as a flash of red on the wall caught his eye. Backing up, he stared at the fire alarm for a moment, considering the possibilities. Not only would it clear out the rooms here, it would bring security, leaving the office either empty or light on personnel. Shoving his keys back into his pocket, he raised his arm, pulled the sleeve of his leather jacket tight, and brought his elbow down hard on the glass rod, sprinting back down the hall to hide in the small staff room beside the elevator.

He watched people run past from behind a huge fake tree, grateful when he saw the woman from the other night enter the stairwell, a baby-sized bundle in her arms. Some wouldn't leave, he knew, but she was the important one. Slipping down the now-quiet hall, he inserted his master key in the lock for room 312 and let himself in, shutting the door as quietly as possible. Moving cautiously lest a bodyguard had been left behind, he searched the rooms, looking for anything that would tell him where the next meet was supposed to be.

The fire alarm quieted. Damn. It was too quick for the fire department to have arrived, which meant the security guys must have figured out his ruse. He stood in the doorway to the bedroom, taking one last look. He'd have to go across the hall, if he still could...

His gaze landed on a tiny rounded edge of metal barely peeking out from under the bed. Frowning, he jogged over and pulled it out. A cell phone. His luck had just changed. Checking the calendar, he found a drop off scheduled for three in the afternoon with a "Mr. & Mrs. Jones". How original.

Pushing the phone into his jeans pocket, he went for the door, only to hear a key being fitted in the lock. He ran back into the bedroom & pushed the window open, climbing out on a narrow ledge. Stretching out with his foot, he pushed the window shut and then scooted along the brick until he reached a metal roof access ladder. He climbed down as quickly as possible, grateful for the early morning darkness as he ran into the trees and made his way across the compound to the security office.

As expected, security seemed light as one lone guard wandered back and forth at the back of the building. Through the windows, two more large silhouettes were moving within. Harley didn't need to get into the building itself, just a small shed about a hundred yards away where the old equipment was kept. As long as everyone stayed where they were, he should be able to sneak in and out without being detected.

Keeping to the cover of trees, he moved around the perimeter as the first streaks of light started to appear in the sky. He crouched low just behind the shed, sneaking slowly around the corner and up the side. Peeking around to the front door, he noted that the padlock was missing, and for once he was grateful he hadn't had time to replace it. The guard turned his back, and Harley sprinted for the shed door, just barely closing it behind him as he saw the guard turn again through the dirty window.

It was dark, but Harley knew what he was looking for. He felt his way down the shelves to the very back of the shed, and took a small box from where he'd left it months ago. He tucked it under his arm like a football, and went back to the door, letting himself out the same way he'd gone in. As the sun started to come up over the horizon, he took out his cell phone and dialed the harem.

"Veronica Rowan, please." He waited for her to pick up, scowling when no one answered. His heart racing, he jogged between buildings to the Double D. Where could they have gone? A million scenarios raced through his mind as he opened the cellar door and descended into the warren of tunnels once more. He grabbed a flashlight at the entrance and jogged toward the harem, dreading what he'd find when he got there.

* * *

"Who is he?" Monica asked, careful to keep her voice low. Veronica and one of the other girls had shown her a few easy ways to get loose if someone grabbed her, and on the way out of the gym the harem girl had paused, her attention drawn to a man working on a piece of equipment across the room. He already had an audience of three other giggling beauties, and Veronica shook her head, turning back to the door.

"That's Chance, the handyman. As you can see he's quite...popular." She pulled Monica into the hall. "We'd better get back to my dressing room before Harley figures out I forgot my phone. There will be hell to pay if he's looking for you."

Monica hurried behind her, grinning at the way Veronica had changed the subject. "So you and Chance..."

"No." She fitted the key in her lock then held the door open for Monica. "I don't date guys bigger than me," she clarified, still holding the door open. She smiled wryly, winking at Monica as footsteps pounded down the hall toward them. "Not quick enough, I guess." Harley skidded to a stop in front of the door just then, breathing heavily as Monica raised an eyebrow at him.

"Miss me?"

In two steps he was in front of her, dropping a box to the floor as he pulled her tight to his chest. His lips descended, delivering a punishing, possessive kiss that made Monica's head spin. She grasped Harley's neck, running her fingers through his hair as she gave him the reassurance he obviously sought. When he pulled back, he glanced over his shoulder at Veronica.

"Why didn't you answer the phone? I thought something happened..."

Monica reached up and turned his head to face her. "We just forgot the phone is all. Veronica was showing me a few protection moves in the gym, and--"

Harley frowned and stepped back, leaving Monica to miss the warm contact. "You left this room? I told you to stay here. What if someone had seen you?" He turned around. "And what were you thinking, taking her out there, showing her moves? She's got a gash in her head, dammit - what the hell were you thinking?"

"Whoa." Veronica put both hands up. "I was thinking she needed to stay awake, and this little room wasn't cutting it. Laura and I demonstrated some moves for her - she didn't actually do anything but watch. And you never said not to leave the room. So just cool it. Everyone's fine."

Monica saw Harley's fists clench. Apparently Veronica did too, judging from her tense muscles and the way she tried to back up. Only there was no where to go, and she pressed herself tight against the door, eyes narrowed in a cold stare. Monica stepped in front of Harley, putting a hand in the center of his chest.

"That's enough. Calm down, both of you. I'm fine, nothing happened. Did you get what we need, hon?"

At the endearment, he looked down, the tension slowly leaving his body as he nodded. He glanced over her shoulder. "You and I will talk later." Looking down at Monica, he bent to pick up the box he'd dropped earlier, and grabbed her hand. "We have to go. Now."

Veronica opened the door, standing well away as he pulled her forward. Monica shrugged as she went past, relieved when Veronica winked at her. The door closed and she jogged after Harley down a long hallway and two flights of stairs into a dark basement. He unlocked a door underneath the stairwell and ushered her into the tunnels once again.

Chapter Thirteen

"You scared her," Monica said a couple minutes later, following Harley down the cold, dark passage. Her nose wrinkled at the strong, earthy scent, more prominent here than in the other tunnels. The walls seemed closer too, and the flashlight beam barely illuminated the rough path ahead. She shivered.

"It isn't the first time, and probably won't be the last," Harley said, never breaking stride. "She can handle it."

Monica stumbled over an uneven patch of earth, reaching one hand out to steady herself on the wall. The surface was sharper than she'd anticipated and she felt the rock dig into her skin. "Ow." She wiped her hand on her jeans, walking right into Harley's back when he stopped short. "I just don't think she should have to handle it. You didn't have to be so--"

"So what?" He turned, holding the flashlight up

like a torch, providing too little light to do any good. "I've known Veronica a lot longer than you, darlin', and she'd be insulted if I changed on account of her." He played the light over Monica's body, scanning up one side and down the other. "What was 'ow'?"

She shook her head. "Just a scrape on my hand, nothing important." She held her hand out, palm up so he could inspect it, surprised when he put the box he held on the floor so he could hold her fingers steady. Nervous, she shifted from one foot to the other, his silence putting all sorts of bad thoughts about what might be on the wall in her head. "I tripped, and used the wall to keep from falling. Is that okay? Something I should know?"

He raised her hand to his lips, placing a gentle kiss in the center. "No, sorry. I should have warned you the tunnel walls are rougher on this side of the ranch. We haven't done anything with these just because of how different the rock is here. You're okay then?"

She laughed. "Of course. I'm fine. Really." He leaned closer, and for a moment she thought he might kiss her, but he bent to pick up the small box, and turned to start walking again. "What's in the box?" she asked, paying close attention to the ground as she followed.

"Old surveillance stuff." He paused, leading her into a side tunnel that felt even smaller than the first one had. "I got a video recorder and a voice recorder - just in case the video fails for some reason. They're both digital, so when we're done we can just take the whole thing to the authorities." He stopped in front of a metal ladder attached to a wall, and shined the flashlight overhead. Monica could see a square wooden door above.

"We're going up here?"

Harley nodded, handing her the box. "Let me climb up and make sure there's nothing over the door." The ladder wasn't very long, and Harley was pushing the wooden slabs up soon after. Monica expected to see light from the crack he opened up, but it was just more darkness. Harley shoved hard, and one side of the door flew up and to the side. He reached down for the box and then climbed up the rest of the way. Thirty seconds later Monica climbed up into a very tidy storage room lined with shelves and racks of clothing.

Swinging the door back into place, Harley secured it. "This way," he said, moving to a door at the far end of the room. He pulled it open and bright, blinding light streamed in. Blinking hard, Monica squinted, unable to see a thing.

"It's about time you guys got here," a low, unfamiliar voice rumbled.

Monica stepped into the brightness after Harley, the door behind her closing with a loud click. Her eyes gradually adjusted, and when she could finally see again Harley was shaking hands with yet another tall, rugged-looking guy with a killer jaw line. She shook her head, earning confused looks from both men.

"Monica, this is Alex. He manages the salon for me, and does massage, hair, makeup, and nails. Today he's our costume and makeover guru." Harley took her hand, pulling her forward.

She held her other hand out and smiled. "Nice to meet you, Alex. I wasn't expecting someone so--"

"Not gay?" He grinned, winking at Harley. "I get that a lot. The ladies don't seem to mind though."

She shook her head, laughing. "That never crossed my mind, actually. You're just so...well...good-looking. And manly. You look like you should be working at the Double D with Harley, not shampooing hair." An image of him bent over a woman's hands, applying polish flitted through her mind, and she couldn't decide if it was sexy or just weird.

Alex led them to a corner of the room set up with two salon chairs, and motioned for them to sit down. "I used to work in Hollywood, actually - a small studio doing costumes and makeup. If it makes you feel better, I worked mostly on horror films. Lots of fake blood and carnage." He winked at her then tilted his head, his eyes turning serious as he examined her from head to toe. Monica felt like squirming under his gaze, but managed to stay still.

"When I met him, the studio had just closed and he was out of work. I offered him the same salary and training if he'd fulfill a few fantasies per day." Harley chuckled. "He didn't put up much of a fight."

Alex ran his fingers over Monica's jaw, turning her head gently right and left. "It's a good gig," he said, releasing her and stepping back with a nod. "I get to make women feel beautiful for a few hours, they're...uh, very grateful, and I get paid for it." He moved to a clothing rack and retrieved a professional-looking gray skirt suit in a clear garment bag. "We'll start you with this. And before you argue, remember you're going undercover. You need to look as little like yourself as possible."

She stood, wrinkling her nose as she accepted the hanger. "Where--"

"Right behind that screen." He pointed behind her to a dark red folding screen with a black frame. She went behind it and changed quickly, listening to the guys bantering like old friends. There was a white silk blouse to go under the jacket, and thigh-high panty hose that she wrestled up her legs, trying to remember the last time she'd worn a pair. Slipping her feet into matching gray pumps, she stepped out from behind the screen, heels clicking on the hard floor.

"You clean up good, Mrs. Majors." Harley stood on the other side of the room in front of a similar screen. He'd changed into a black suit and tie with a blue shirt underneath, and Monica nearly swooned at the sight of those wide shoulders draped in expensive fabric.

"Likewise, Mr. Majors." She started walking toward him, her thigh-highs suddenly feeling very sexy.

Alex stepped between them, holding one hand up at each of them. "Sorry guys. We've still got a long ways to go here, and I've got a client in two hours. Back to your chairs for now. You can rip those clothes off each other later."

Monica stuck out her lower lip and sighed. "Fine. But you're not really helping me fulfill my fantasy." She settled into her chair as Alex covered her with an apron, securing it at her neck.

"Don't worry sweetheart," Harley said, leaning back in his own chair. "I'll make sure your fantasies come true in good time."

* * *

This is going to work. Harley glanced at Monica as they went out the back door of the salon. He wouldn't have recognized her on the street after Alex finished with her. Aside from the prim gray suit and demure shoes, Alex had applied latex with some sort of skin glue and thick make-up to her face and neck, transforming her into an older, almost sickly looking character. The wig she wore was a dark blond color rolled up into a classic twist at the back of her head to fit with the professional attire. Harley was both amazed and frustrated with the transformation. The suit was sexy, the rest just made him feel disoriented.

Monica looked up at him, smiling, though the faux skin kept it from reaching her eyes. "You look so...different," she said, reaching up to almost touch his face before dropping her hand back to her side. "I'm afraid to touch it - wouldn't want to ruin all that hard work."

"The wig itches," he complained, scratching carefully at the back of his neck. "Or it could be all those pins he used to keep my hair under the cap." He had a new appreciation for actors and anyone who had to wear a wig on a regular basis.

She took his hand and laced her fingers through his. "No one will recognize you though, and this will be over soon. What time is the meet?"

"Three this afternoon. We need to get to Reno, find the original clients and get everything set up." He squeezed her hand and pulled away, needing to put his focus back on the project. He pointed to a sleek green car parked a few feet away. "That belongs to the ranch - we'll take it into the city, since it doesn't have any markings. Ready?"

She nodded, falling into step beside him. "As ready as I'm going to get," she said, stepping carefully on the gravel. "I should have kept my tennis shoes for this part."

Harley grinned. "I can carry you if you want." He remembered how she felt in his arms the last time. A perfect fit. Although seeing that cute little ass hanging over his shoulder might be fun too.

She shook her head and cocked one highly plucked eyebrow in mock disapproval. "We wouldn't want to cause a scene, now would we, Mr...ah...what are our names again?"

"Nick and Darcy Benoit. I'm a wealthy oil magnate from Alaska, and you're my trophy wife-slash-office manager."

Monica snorted. "Your buddy has an interesting in- terpretation of 'trophy wife'," she said, sliding into the passenger side of a big green Cadillac sedan. Harley got behind the wheel and put the box of equipment on the seat between them. He reached over and popped another button on Monica's white silk shirt, running his finger over the lacy edge of her bra.

"I think Alex got this one right," he said, feeling her shiver under his touch. "He knows the real prize is what's underneath." Reluctantly he pulled his hand away and started the car, feeling her stare as he pulled onto a back road that would take them out of the ranch. Monica took the box and put it on the floor, scooting closer. He knew he was in trouble when her hand caressed his thigh and then drifted between his legs.

* * *

She stroked her fingers lightly up and down the front of Harley's pants, thrilling at the way his cock jumped to meet her fingers each time. Maybe it was all the makeup, but she felt detached from this altered version of the strong, biker-tough man she loved. She

needed something familiar to reorient herself. To remind herself that she knew him on a more intimate
level than a change in looks and clothing could hide.
Fumbling for his zipper, she was so intent on her task
that she gasped when he grabbed her wrist, hard, and
pulled her hand away.

Looking up at his expressionless face, she tried to
free herself to no avail. She looked away, blinking
back tears. It wasn't just the makeup then. He really
wasn't the same. He held her wrist until he pulled off
the road onto the shoulder, then let her go. She stared
out the window. How appropriate that a thunder-
storm seemed to be moving in.

"Monica, look at me." His voice was gentle, soothing, and she nearly heeded his request.

She shook her head. "It's not you," she said, carefully patting under one eye with a finger. "This whole
costume thing is just weird, is all. I'll get it together,
just give me a minute, okay?"

His warm hand slid over her shoulder, pulling her
toward him. "Come on, sweetheart. Don't look at my
face, look in my eyes."

She didn't fight, trusting him on a level she didn't
quite understand. Her gaze met his and she nearly
leaned back from the intensity in of emotion in his
eyes. "There you are," she whispered, her fingers
lightly touching his neck, his shoulder, his chest before falling back to her lap. "I just..."

"I know," he said, rubbing a hand up and down her

arm. "But this costume thing is one of the last things standing between you and your freedom. Unless you know how to fix whatever we ruin, we're going to have to behave ourselves until after the meet."

She nodded and took a deep breath, letting it out slow and easy. It was followed by a wide yawn that she tried and failed to stifle. "Sorry," she said, shaking it off. "I think I'm just really tired. You must be too - we didn't exactly sleep last night."

Harley put the car back in drive and pulled onto the road again. "I'm not too bad. Why don't you try to get some rest on the way?"

"Are you okay to drive?" she was already leaning back against the seat, her eyelids so heavy it was all she could do to blink at him.

He glanced quickly at her, then looked back at the road, chuckling. "I'm fine. Get some sleep."

The next thing she knew, someone was jiggling her arm.

"Wake up, sleepyhead." Harley's amused voice pulled her out of a rather naughty dream, and she felt her cheeks heat as she opened her eyes to see his smirking face. "That looked like some dream. If we didn't have things to do..."

"Promises, promises," she mumbled and leaned forward, remembering not to rub her face at the last second. "How long was I out?"

He handed her a bottle of water. "It's two-thirty. The Benoits are in that gray house over there." He pointed to a house across the street and several lots down. "You stay here and wake up. I'm going to go knock and leave a note that the meeting place has changed. Hopefully they'll leave right away so we have time to set up. I'll come get you when they're gone."

Chapter Fourteen

Harley walked briskly down the block, his head up and shoulders back to portray a man who knew exactly where he was going and why. When he reached the gray house, he pulled the note he'd scrawled out of his pocket, and knocked on the door exactly three times. It opened almost immediately, a distinguished middle-aged man in a sharp gray jacket that matched his house peering out at him.

He held out the paper. "Message for Mr. Benoit."

The man took it from him, frowning as he scanned the contents. "Darcy!"

Heels clicked purposefully across the hardwood floor as a tall blond with impeccable makeup came into view. "What's wrong? Are they not coming? Did they change their minds? Oh--" She stopped short when she saw Harley. "I'm sorry, I didn't know you had company."

"He's not company." Nick tucked the note in his pocket, then took his wallet out. "Get your purse. The meeting place has changed and we need to leave now if we're going to make it." Darcy disappeared and Nick handed Harley a ten dollar bill. "Thanks," he said, turning away and closing the door. Clearly dismissed, Harley walked down the street, past the car and around the corner, just in case Benoit was watching. He turned up the alley and went back to stand in the bushes adjacent to the Benoit house, watching and listening for any activity. He heard the garage door go up, and then a car started. From his vantage point he could just barely see the side of the Cadillac as it glided out into the street and pulled away.

He picked the back door lock and went inside, making sure there were no alarms or cameras already in place. Leaving the back door unlocked, he went back down the alley and around the corner to where Monica waited in the car.

"They're gone," he said, leaning in the open driver's side window. "Hand me that box, and we'll go in the back. The less people who see us at the front of the house, the better."

She handed the box through the window then rolled it up, locking the car as she got out. "How far did you send them?" They retraced Harley's path up the alley and through the Benoit's back yard.

"Next town over," he said, setting the box on the dining room table. "It's about a thirty minute drive, so by the time they get there and realize they've been scammed, it will take them awhile to get back. Hopefully long enough." He checked his watch. "We've got about fifteen minutes - help me get this camera set up in the living room."

They hid the camera at the base of a large potted tree, and Harley cut a hole in the back of a couch pillow and put a small audio recording device inside aimed at the room. Monica put the box under the kitchen counter, and they took a quick tour so they'd know where everything was. Back in the living room, Harley looked at the clock on the wall, watching the second hand count down to the hour.

At three-o-clock sharp, there was a knock at the door.

Harley glanced at Monica and nodded. He straightened his suit jacket and opened the door, standing back to let the woman from Room 312 back at the ranch in, followed by her bodyguard. The woman carried a car seat covered with a fleece blanket. The man carried a silver briefcase.

Monica stepped forward, and Harley was impressed with the expression of longing she managed as she looked at the bundle hanging from the woman's arm.

"Is that my baby?" she asked, moving closer, a hopeful smile playing at her lips. *Damn*, Harley thought. *She's good.*

The woman swung the carrier neatly out of reach.

"Payment first," she said firmly, nodding toward the man who had opened his case on the entry table.

"I think we should see what we're getting first," Harley said, noting that the bodyguard seemed almost bored with the situation. That was good. The more normal things appeared, the less skittish they'd be.

"You wanted a girl baby, you get a girl baby. Payment first. Those are the terms. Or we can leave."

Harley stroked his chin, looking over her head and out the window. A black sedan was parked outside and he could just make out a person sitting in the passenger seat. Burns had come along after all then, overseeing this drop personally. That would make things a lot easier.

"I think if that baby was healthy, you'd have no problem showing me the merchandise, so to speak," Harley said, looking down at the woman. "I think there must be something wrong that you don't want us to know about."

"Nothing's wrong with the kid." The gruff tone from the bodyguard told Harley he was pressing the right buttons. Just a few more, and hopefully they'd call Burns in.

He turned to face the bodyguard. "Why should I trust you? You just want money. I want to be sure I have a healthy child." He looked over his shoulder at Monica. "I don't think this is a good idea, honey. I don't trust them."

"Just give them a quick look," the bodyguard said,

frustration in his voice. "Let's get this done already."

"But we're not supp--"

"Just do it."

The woman reluctantly set the carrier on the couch and removed the blanket. Nestled in another blanket lay a small child with a shock of dark hair already on her head. She was sleeping, and Monica leaned in for a closer look while Harley stood back and watched. Would she do that with their child someday?

Monica straightened, looking at him with an un-readable expression. "There's a bruise on her arm," she said, wringing her hands in front of her. "It's fad-ing, but--"

High-pitched beeps drew their attention to the bodyguard, punching numbers on his phone. He held the device to his ear. "We might have a problem. There's a bruise on the kid's arm." He hesitated, then nodded. "Okay." Disconnecting the call he pushed the phone back into his pocket and went to the door. "The boss wants to verify for himself."

Harley suppressed a grin as the man opened the door, and Stephen Burns walked into the trap.

* * *

Monica avoided Burns' eyes as he walked in. Clasp-ing her hands in front of her, she willed them to stop shaking. Harley didn't so much as glance her way, but reached out to shake Burns' hand. Burns ignored it, brushing past Harley to take the baby out of the carrier and hold her up at arms length.

"You said there was a bruise on her arm?" He frowned, turning the now-fidgeting child this way and that. "Show me."

Monica stepped up and pointed, her eyes meeting Harley's over Burns' arms. He'd thought she made it up, judging from the look on his face.

"Mmm-hmm." Burns turned and handed the child back to the nanny. "It's a pretty small thing - and kids do get bruised occasionally, but you wouldn't know that, of course." His patronizing tone grated on Monica's nerves, but she managed to remain silent as he continued. "How about we knock off three percent of the price for damaged goods. This will be my last deal for awhile, and I'm feeling generous."

Harley stroked his chin, appearing to consider it. "I was thinking more like five percent," he said. "Don't want the neighbors thinking we beat up on our kid."

"Four percent."

Harley smiled as if that was what he wanted all along. "Done." He handed a credit card to the man behind him then rubbed his hands together. "So are you taking a vacation or retiring?"

The baby started crying, and the nanny handed her off to Monica. "You may as well start now," she said, taking the bag off her shoulder and setting it on the couch. That's the diaper bag, and there are some diapers in the side pocket."

"Thank you," Monica said, pitching her voice lower than normal. "I'll just take her too her room..."

Burns held a hand up. "Did that payment go through yet?" The bodyguard nodded once, and Burns dropped his arm. "That's fine then. Enjoy your new baby, ma'am."

She nodded and put the diaper bag over her shoulder, keeping her eyes downcast as she carried the baby down the hall. Leaving the door open she changed the child as quickly as she could, thankful for the few babysitting jobs she'd had as a teen. Putting the baby in the crib, she went back to the door and tried to hear the conversation from the living room, but the voices were too soft.

Noting the child was sleeping again, she decided to leave the girl there, where she'd be safe if anything happened. Closing the door behind her, she walked back down the hall, unsure whether she should join the others, or wait until Burns and his people were gone. It was odd they hadn't left yet. They had the money. Maybe something was wrong.

She stepped into the living room just as the front door burst open. A man came through the doorway, his face tight with anger as he surveyed the scene.

"What the hell is going on? Who are you people, and what are you doing in our house?"

* * *

A woman shrieked just outside the open front door as Burns pulled a gun and leveled it at the man Monica presumed was Nick Benoit. Benoit put his hands up, and Harley's gaze darted to the hall, found her and nodded slightly toward the kitchen. She moved through the doorway, staying close to the wall but the bodyguard spotted her, pointing his own gun her way.

"Hold it right there," he said, the command causing both Benoit and Burns to look in her direction. Harley slammed his body into Burns' back, catching the man off guard and sending him toppling into Benoit. In turn, Benoit fell into the bodyguard, hard enough to knock him against the hall table. The jumble forced him to lower his hands and the gun to keep from falling, but it was clear he'd recover quickly.

"Head's up," Harley called, tossing her the pillow from the couch as he swept his fingers down into the plant pot to retrieve the camera. In two long strides he was beside her, pulling her through the kitchen and out the back door. A loud pop rang in Monica's ears, and she heard something whizz by, but didn't feel anything and Harley didn't break stride. They reached the car in seconds and hopped in, Harley peeling away from the curb in a squeal of rubber on asphalt.

"Get the recorder out of the pillow," he said, turning left, then right just a few yards later, his eyes constantly darting to the rear view mirror. She did as he asked, tossing the pillow in the back seat and shoving the small audio device into one of her front pockets. She grabbed the camera off the seat and disconnected the cord, putting that in her other pocket, all the while trying to stay upright as Harley tried to lose the car following them.

"Just lay down on the seat," he said, taking another sharp corner. "It will be safer that way. If I can just..."

She ducked down, bracing her feet under the dash as she grasped the seat with both hands. It seemed like forever until he slowed down, and his knuckles were white on the steering wheel when he finally brought the car to a stop. He turned the engine off, then breathed for a few seconds before he looked down at her.

"You okay?"

She nodded, pushing herself up on the seat and looking around. They were in an alley of some sort, both sides lined with thick concrete block buildings. "Fine, I think," she said, turning back to him. His face was pale, and she frowned, reaching out to feel his skin. It was cold and clammy. "But you're not. What's --" she finally noticed the red staining the seat beside him. "Oh no. You have to get to a hospital. Let me drive - tell me where to go..." She reached behind her for the door handle, but he caught her other wrist, pulling her back with more strength than she would have expected.

"I'll be fine. You need to get that information to

the FBI. Burns probably already has the police out looking for us, and who knows what he's told them by now." He took a deep breath, then let it out, and glanced toward the back seat. "The black bag has a change of clothes and some money. The bus station is just on the other side of this wall. Get on the next bus out of town, and go to the field office in Las Vegas. Tell them everything, and give them the evidence. Bring them back to the ranch."

She shook her head, blinking at the tears gathering in her eyes. "I can't just leave you here - not like this. Not by yourself. I won't. I'm not running away again."

He reached out to cup the side of her face, wincing at the motion. "You're not running away. You'll be back soon, and Burns will go to jail, and you can be free. Just like you wanted." He tugged her forward and she went willingly, his lips meeting hers for a quick, gentle kiss. "Go on now. I'll get this stitched up back at the ranch. It will all work out, trust me."

She nodded, swiping at escaped tears as she caught her breath. "I do," she said, squeezing his hand one last time. "I'll be back as soon as I can. Promise."

Forcing herself to pull away from Harley's touch, she wished she could see his face - his real face - one last time before she left. But there was no time. She grabbed the bag from the back seat and shut the door, hesitating for a few more seconds before finally walking away, her heart tearing in two.

She almost looked back at the corner of the building, but didn't allow herself the luxury. If she was going to do this, she had to just go. Just like every other time. Only it wasn't. Because this time, she was coming back.

Ducking into the restroom she locked herself in the handicapped stall and undid all of Alex's careful work. Most of it she stuffed in the trash, but she carefully rolled the suit and shirt to pack back in the bag, replacing the jeans, sweatshirt and tennis shoes Harley had packed. He must have known all along she'd be going alone, since all the clothing was in her size. The thought made her mad, and as she counted out a few bills to put in her pocket from the cash he'd included, she vowed to give him a piece of her mind about that.

When she got back.

Checking the mirror for any stray bits of faux flesh she might have missed, she rinsed her face, pulled her hair up into a pony tail and went out to the ticket counter. "One for the next bus to Vegas, please. Round trip."

Chapter Fifteen

As soon as Monica disappeared from view, Harley eased out of his suit jacket, balling the expensive material up and pressing hard against his side. Reaching up with the other arm, he opened the compartment in the roof for sunglasses and took out his cell phone, punching in the ranch clinic's number for the second time that day.

"Doc? It's Harley. How are your bullet hole skills?" He held the phone away from his ear, the string of curses coming out of the receiver bringing a tight grin to his lips. When it grew quiet, he tried again. "If you're finished, I'll be there in half an hour or so. Meet me in the tunnel." More yelling, and Harley chuckled as he disconnected the call, then winced again at the fire in his side. Ben Martin was a bit rough around the edges, but he was a good doctor, and if anyone could fix this, he could. As long as Harley could get himself back to the ranch.

He checked his watch, but knew he couldn't wait any longer. Securing the jacket tight to his side with the seatbelt, he started the ignition and slowly pulled out of the alley, peering into the station window, his eyes searching the loose crowd. He scanned right past her at first then looked back. There she was, by the vending machine, all cleaned up and looking right at him. She held up her ticket and looked up as if she was listening to something. One last little wave and she turned away, walking toward the boarding area in back.

Good. She was safe, for a while at least. He breathed a sigh of relief, pulling away from the curb to take a zigzag route to the highway.

By the time he was within a mile of the turnoff for the tunnels, he was struggling hard to stay awake, and decided he'd be better off on foot. Pulling off the road, he drove into the trees far enough the car wouldn't be noticeable, and tied the jacket around his waist to keep the pressure on his wound. Ten minutes later, he wished he'd kept the car as he stopped to rest against a gnarled tree trunk. He dug the phone out of his pocket to check the time. It had been forty minutes since he called Ben. Hopefully the doctor would be worried enough to come looking for him. He stumbled on, stopping every thirty feet or so to rest, and when the tangled vines that marked the tunnel entrance finally came into view, he'd never been so happy in his life. They'd done it. Monica had the evidence, she'd get it to the FBI, and he'd hide out underground until she came back with the cavalry. Limping forward, he pulled the door open, glad to see Ben standing there, waiting with a gurney just behind him.

"Thank god you're here," Harley heard himself say, though it sounded like someone else's voice. "I don't think I could have made it the rest of the way without you."

Strangely quiet, Ben stepped up and slid an arm around him, helping him onto the gurney. When he was strapped in and covered with a blanket, Ben leaned down and mouthed the words, "I'm sorry."

The last thing Harley saw before he passed out was Stephen Burns, grinning down at him.

* * *

The next time Harley opened his eyes, he was in one of the small patient rooms at the clinic. Shifting slightly, he winced at the pain in his side. Lifting the blanket, he felt a bandage under the thin gown covering his side where Ben must have stitched him up.

"He's awake."

Harley dropped the blanket back in place and looked at the man sitting just inside his door. "I take it you're the warden," he said, pressing a button on the side of his bed to raise himself to a sitting position. It hurt more than he thought it would, and he cringed again as the door opened and Burns walked in, Ben trailing behind.

"Well, well," Burns said, walking right up to the bed. "So it was you under all that makeup. And I suppose that was Monica with you earlier. I should have known." He leaned over the bed rail as Ben came around to the other side. "Where is my daughter, by the way? I thought I asked you to look after her. I have to say, you're doing a piss-poor job, son."

Harley groaned as the heel of Burns' hand pressed into his wounded side. Ben reached for Burns then stopped as one of the guards released the safety on a gun pointed at his head. Burns rocked back, taking the pressure with him and Harley gulped for air as he fought the pain. Adrenaline coursed through his body, and it was all he could do to stay still.

"I haven't got all day," Burns said, holding his hand out again.

Harley lifted his hands in mock surrender. "She left," he said, coughing lightly. "I don't know where she went, but she's not coming back. Ever." In that moment, he wished it was true. She shouldn't come back to face this, it was too dangerous. He should have sent her farther away. Looking Burns in the eye, he steeled himself for the pain he knew was coming. "If it's the evidence you want, you're out of luck. I mailed it to the FBI in DC. I bet they'll come looking for you before the weekend comes. And Monica will be far, far away. You lose, Burns."

The attack he was expecting never came. Instead,
Burns just stood back and clapped, smiling. "Well
done," he said, taking his cell phone out of his pocket.
"I was hoping you wouldn't give up too easily. But
her intentions are irrelevant." He touched the screen a
few times then held the device out for Harley to see.
"The first time she ran off, my men had to drug her
to bring her back. I had a microchip implanted in her
shoulder in case it ever happened again. As you can
see, it was a worthwhile investment."

Harley watched a red dot move along a map on the
small screen, everything falling into place. Monica had
said they always found her, no matter how careful she
was. A blue dot appeared at the bottom of the screen,
following the same route, and Harley gripping the
railing tightly as the dots grew closer together.

"You son of a bitch."

Burns turned the phone to look, and nodded.
"That will be Doug," he said, looking back up at Harley. "I must admit, while this little game was fun at
first, I've grown weary of chasing my daughter all
over the country. It's expensive. Since she refuses to
abide by my wishes, my only option is to punish her
in a way that will ensure her future obedience." He
put the phone in his pocket and walked to the door,
pausing just outside.

"I'll let you know when she gets back. I'm sure
she'll want to say goodbye."

After he closed the door, Harley closed his eyes and took a deep breath. He needed to be ready when Monica got back. No way was that monster going to get away with whatever he had planned. When he opened his eyes, Ben was still at his side. He passed him a couple pills and a glass of water, and then Harley felt him slip something small and metal under the blanket near his thigh. Harley handed him the empty glass, and nodded as Ben took it and left the room.

Monica stretched and rubbed the back of her neck with one hand as she stepped off the bus in Salt Lake City. When she'd bought the ticket, she'd been dismayed that there was no direct route to Las Vegas, and that the one-way trip would take up to twenty hours. She needed to transfer to a different bus, but as she made her way across the dimly lit terminal, a sign on a large bulletin board caught her eye. It was an FBI "Wanted" poster, with the address of a local field office listed on the bottom. Thinking for a moment, she tried to remember if Burns had any connections in Utah, but couldn't think of any that she knew of. The chances were probably just as likely as Vegas, and if she could just hole up somewhere for the rest of the night, she could be at the office first thing in the morning.

The decision made, she punched the address into

her cell phone, and brought up directions for how to get there. Of course it would be all the way across the city. She glanced at the time - ten o'clock. All the rental places would be closed by now, which left her either on foot, or in a cab. Easy choice.

Shifting her bag to the other hand, she walked out to the curb, giving several transient-looking people a wide berth. She walked half-a-block down and looked both ways, surprised not to see cabs lined up along the curb. Apparently bus travelers weren't big enough business to warrant a presence. Noting more traffic at one of the cross streets ahead, she hiked up to the corner and looked around, watching at least two cabs go by. When the next one came by, she held up a hand, grateful when it pulled to the curb.

"257 East 200 South please," she said as she got in the back seat. The driver, a man who appeared to be in his late forties frowned over the seat at her.

"Nothing's open over there this time of night. You sure you got the right address?"

She nodded. "I'm sure. Thank you."

He shook his head and faced forward again, muttering something under his breath as he pulled away from the curb. She looked out the window as they drove, wondering where Harley was now. Hopefully he'd gotten to the doctor in time, and was somewhere safe to heal. Tears pricked her eyes as she pushed the other options out of her mind. He had to be okay. She couldn't stand to think that something might have happened to him.

Pulling out her phone, she dialed Harley's number. It was risky, she knew, but she just wanted to know he was okay. To hear his voice again. Holding the phone to her ear, she waited as it rang back at her twice before his voice mail picked up. She left a quick but vague message and hung up. Just in case.

Stifling a yawn, she laid her head back on the seat. Maybe she'd just take a quick nap to refresh herself. Her eyes drifted shut and just as she felt herself dosing off, the car lurched forward, tossing her forward into the Plexiglas window. Her head bounced off the thick plastic and she fell back on the seat, dazed as the car came to an abrupt stop.

She'd barely pushed herself to a seated position when the back door of the cab opened. Strong hands grabbed her arm, yanking her out of the vehicle. She kicked at her would-be captor, punching with her free arm until he threw her to the ground and put one knee in her back. Behind them, an engine roared, and metal squealed against metal. Turning her head to the side, she saw the cab sped away. Cold metal slapped around her wrists as the man cuffed her, hauling her to her feet.

"Your father's been looking for you," he said, his voice softer than she would have imagined. He pulled her to a large black SUV and helped her into the passenger seat. "If you'll just tell me where the recording devices are, we can pick those up on the way back to the ranch."

"They--" Monica stopped, realizing the bag was still in the cab. It was dark, and the bag had been on the floor at her feet. She hadn't thought to grab it while she was being manhandled. Maybe if she could get away, she could find the cab...though the chances of finding the right one in a city this large was practically nil. But it was the only evidence they had. Without it, all of this had been for nothing, and Burns would win.

"Well?"

She looked up into eyes that weren't as cold as those she normally encountered in Burns' men. "Why do you do it?" she asked. He stepped back, the question appearing to have caught him off guard. "Why do you work for my--Burns, when you could be doing something...else?"

He shrugged, looking off into the distance. "We all make choices. Every choice has a price." Turning back to her, he rested his forearm on the frame above her head. "Your father's heart is in the right place, even if his execution is questionable. You'd do well to remember you might not be alive if it weren't for him. Now tell me where we need to go to get the video, and we'll get going."

She looked down at her knees, as if he'd won. "The bus station," she said, shifting in the seat as though she couldn't get comfortable. "I put them in a locker." There were lots of people at the station all night long.

That would be her best bet at getting free so she could find the cab.

"Where's the key?"

Damn. She shifted again, hoping he'd take the hint and unlock the cuffs. "I hid it in one of the planters outside, so I wouldn't lose it."

He closed the door and walked around to the driver's side, sliding behind the wheel. The automatic locks clicked into place as he pushed a button on his door. "Turn around." She did, relieved when he removed the metal from her wrists.

He started the engine and turned the car around, taking her back toward the depot as she rubbed her wrists. Glancing over at him, she thought about what he'd said. He was right that she might not be alive without Burns...but she just couldn't get around the fact that her father was buying and selling human beings. Surely that was wrong no matter what the motivation behind it. There had to be other, legal means of helping those children. Especially for someone with Burns' wealth. A way that didn't involve large sums of money changing hands...

Every choice has a price. "You bought a child, didn't you?" She watched him closely, his grip tightening on the wheel though his expression remained neutral. "And you're working off the cost."

Chapter Sixteen

Her captor's silence was all the answer Monica needed. How many of the people currently working with Burns were in the same situation? It was a genius move on his part, she thought as they neared the bus station. Fear of losing a child would be good motivation for keeping Burns and his business well-protected.

The SUV came to a stop in a parking space a little ways off from the depot. The man got out and came around to open her door. "Put your hands out," he said, the cuffs dangling from his fingers.

"Is that really necessary?" she asked, slowly lifting her arms. "What will people think?"

He snapped the restraints in place then pulled her out of the vehicle. Keeping one hand on the chain between her wrists, he opened the back door and took out a black leather jacket, threading it over her hands. "Keep that over your hands."

She frowned. "Or what?"

"Or I may tell your father you had an unfortunate accident." He pressed a button on his keys to lock the vehicle, then took her upper arm and propelled her toward the building. "Now, which planter is that key in?"

Monica scanned the layout, trying to decide where her best chance of escape would be. She hadn't counted on the handcuffs, but she had to try. If she couldn't recover the evidence from the cab, she and Harley were as good as dead.

She pointed to a couple of extra-large pots that stood on a narrow stone platform a few feet off the ground. "It's that gold one, on the right. I tossed them up there." She'd have to climb up to peer inside, and there was only enough room for one person. If she could jump off the other side fast enough, she might have a chance at outrunning this guy. Or at least getting to the depot where she could lose him in the transfer area.

Glancing up at him, she could see him thinking about the problems. He could climb up himself, but then she'd be left alone on the ground, which would give her a head start. Though she wouldn't complain if that's how he wanted to play it.

When they reached the spot, she looked at him, trying to appear obedient and docile. "Should I go get them, or do you want to?" He tried to reach a hand up to feel around in the pot, but could only feel about an inch inside the lip.

"Go ahead."

She stifled a grin as she reached out to steady herself on the bench, but couldn't get the leverage she needed with the jacket in the way, and her arms pulled together. "I can't climb up like this, sorry. I guess you'll have to get it."

He thought for a moment. Finally admitting defeat, he took the jacket and quickly unlocked the cuffs. "Get it and come right back down. No funny stuff, or you'll regret it." He stepped back and she boosted herself up on the platform, making a show of digging through the dirt in the pot as she glanced down at him every few seconds.

An elderly man approached, and she smiled and waved as he stopped in front of the man. She heard the stranger ask for directions, and her captor turned away to point down the street. Taking that as her cue, Monica jumped down behind the bench as quietly as she could, and raced into the station.

* * *

Harley slid the slim phone Ben had slipped him under his thigh, and waited. It was probably too late, but he had to warn Monica about the microchip, just in case there was still time for her to get away. If she could get the chip out, she might have a chance.

Stifling the urge to glance at the guard, he forced himself to be still. The man had been on duty for several hours now, barely moving from his chair by the door. He'd have to get up soon, Harley was sure of it. He rotated his own men through four hour shifts for that very reason. Just a few minutes were all he needed, enough to make a quick call. He'd already sent a text, but she hadn't answered. She probably hadn't recognized the number though, and the two words he'd managed to key in - "microchip shoulder" - might have been too cryptic.

The guard shifted, retrieving his phone from his pocket. He slid his thumbs across the screen a few times then glanced up at Harley who closed his eyes and rolled to the side, facing away from the door. Apparently it was enough to satisfy the guard, judging from the sound of the door opening, then closing again with a firm click. Peeking over his shoulder to make sure he was alone, Harley quickly keyed in Monica's number and propped the phone between the pillow and his head. It rang twice, and then the line opened with a click.

"Who is this?" Monica whispered, sounding out of breath. But the fact that she answered gave him hope. Engine noise in the background suggested she must be outside.

"It's Harley. Are you okay?"

She didn't answer for a long moment, and then finally the background noise died away, leaving only the sound of her breathing. "Harley? Thank god - I was so worried!" She took in a big breath then let it out, breathing slower. "I'm...kind of in trouble here. One of Burns' guys found me, and wanted me to give up the equipment. I tricked him and ran away, but he's following me. I can't seem to shake him..."

"I don't have much time, darlin'. There's a micro-chip in your shoulder - that's how he keeps tracking you. I'll explain later, but right now you need to get it out somehow. It's the only way you can lose him."

"No shit."

Harley grinned at the expletive, wishing he was there. She was adorable when she was all fired up. The door knob rattled behind him, wiping the smile off his face. "Listen, I have to go. I'm sorry. But get that chip out and get as far away from here as you can. Don't worry about me, just run. I love you."

He hung up before she could respond, a huge lump in his throat at the thought of never seeing her again. It was better this way though. Keeping her safe was the only thing that mattered.

"Hey, what are you doing over there?" A new voice, a new guard. He rolled to his back, slipping the phone back under his thigh as if he had an itch. The guard stood near the foot of the bed, his hip braced on the frame.

"Same as always," he said, looking the guard in the eye. "Just laying here, getting stronger so I can kick your boss's ass."

The guard's expression remained neutral. "Just keep your hands where I can see them."

"It's not my hands you need to worry about," Harley replied, kicking out with his left foot and catching the man right in the groin.

* * *

"How do I get the chip out? Harley? Oh god." Monica just stared at the phone in her hand, shock and fatigue making it difficult to process the last few seconds. Burns had Harley, which was obvious, but how? A microchip in her shoulder? All this time, and she'd never had a chance. Even now she could hear footsteps coming nearer to the window of the old warehouse she'd ducked into. If what Harley had said about a chip was true, it wouldn't do any good to run. Burns' man would just find her again.

She reached up with her right hand to feel the skin on her left shoulder. Pressing hard, she covered as much area as she could, but it all felt normal. Suppressing a panicked sob as the footsteps stopped, she pressed deeper under the old desk and quickly examined her right shoulder the same way.

Yes.

There was a tiny lump high on her shoulder blade that definitely covered something hard. That had to be it. She heard the man searching just outside the office she was in, moving boxes and shuffling things around. Reaching up, she blindly moved her hand over the desktop, grabbing several long, thin objects in the hope that one would be useful. The pen and pencil were out - she didn't want to poison herself. The third item turned out to be a letter opener with a nice, sharp edge. Perfect.

Wiping off the blade as well as possible on her shirt, she took a deep breath, and worked the metal tip into her skin. Tendrils of pain shot down her arm and she bit her lip to keep quiet, opening the wound enough to get her fingernails in. Grasping the object tight, she exhaled, then took another breath and held it as she yanked it free as she let out her breath in one big gasp.

The noise from the other room stopped and she knew it was over. He'd find her any minute. The pain receded as fresh adrenaline flooded her system, and she pulled herself out from under the desk, taking stock of her surroundings as she turned to face the door. There was a window at her back. That was probably her best chance at getting out.

A large shape loomed in the doorway, the illumination from his cell phone striking Monica as garish. She backed slowly to the window, wincing as she tried to pry the window open. It wouldn't budge. The man turned his phone outwards, and she blinked, holding her hands up to shield her eyes.

"Nice try," he said in that patient tone that was starting to irritate her. "I assume from the blood that you found the chip your father tagged you with?"

She looked down at her hands. She'd wiped them off as well as she could, but even in the inadequate light they looked like the hands of a killer.

"You assume correctly," she said, shivering slightly as the adrenaline began to wear off. She didn't have time for chit chat. She needed to get out now, before shock set in completely. "I'd return it, but that doesn't seem right, somehow." She ground the heel of her foot into the concrete floor. "I bet he'll have a harder time tracking me without it. That seems more sporting anyway."

He laughed. "What makes you think you're getting away this time? We don't need the chip if we have you."

"You don't have me yet." Monica shoved hard against the desk, thankful when it proved to be lighter than it looked. As it went flying toward the shocked man, she flung herself backwards into the window, hoping it would break like they did in the movies.

It didn't.

She dropped to the floor, dull pain suffusing through her shoulder and across her torso as she fought to stay conscious. *Get up. Run.* Somehow she pushed off the floor, closing her eyes while waiting for the latest wave of pain to pass. When she opened them, he was there, standing right in front of her and blocking the only exit.

"Let's go." His phone rang, and he held up a hand,

answering the call with the other. "Doug here. Yeah, she's here. Just caught up with her, actually. I don't think the chip's going to work much longer though. She dug it out." He wrapped a hand around her arm, tugging her back through the dark warehouse with scary accuracy. She twisted and pulled, but couldn't manage to get free. "I'll do that," he said then disconnected the call and turned his phone to use as a flashlight again. When they got to the warehouse door, he stopped and turned to face her.

"Your father--"

"He's not my father."

The man shook his head. "Your father said to tell you that your husband will pay for every hour that it takes you to return to the compound. If you want to spare him as much pain as possible, we'd better leave now."

Monica considered that for a moment. If she didn't get that bag back, there was no other way to prove that Burns was trafficking children. But how could she run knowing that Harley was being tortured and used against her?

Doug led her out the door and helped her into his SUV. She blinked back tears, knowing what she had to do when she spied the keys dangling from the ignition. As soon as he shut the door, she pushed the button to lock herself in and slid over into the driver's seat. Turning the key, she put the car into drive as he fervently punched at the keypad on the door. Just as the locks disengaged, she stabbed at the lock button again and stepped on the gas pedal, punching it nearly to the floor. The vehicle lurched forward, tossing Doug to the side, and flinging her backwards as she peeled out of the alley.

She veered side to side as she tried to gain control of the wheel. Easing up on the fuel she turned onto the main road and started back toward the FBI offices for the second time that night. She'd ditch the vehicle several blocks away and wait for the offices to open. Maybe the FBI could find her bag and the evidence. In the meantime, she'd try not to think about what horrible things Burns could be doing to the man she loved.

Chapter Seventeen

Harley stuffed the unconscious guard into the bathroom and pulled the door shut, wiring it closed with a hanger from the wardrobe. Trying to ignore the pain in his side from the bullet wound, he got the cell phone from the bed and dialed Ben's number. The doctor answered on the second ring.

"Ben? You there?"

"You shouldn't be out of bed in your condition, Mr. Majors." Burns said, mock censure in his tone. "But I'm assuming you are, since my guard hasn't taken your cell phone away. Whose phone is that, Majors? I didn't recognize the number."

Harley closed the cupboard door and moved a panel on the back wall to reveal a tunnel entrance. There was nothing he could do for Ben now except to get a weapon and come back. Hopefully it wouldn't be too late.

He disconnected the call and slid through the small opening, sliding the panel back in place as he heard his hospital room being breached. Standing up, he turned, holding the phone up for light. A tall figure blocked his path, arms crossed over his chest, chuckling.

"Surely you didn't think Burns was stupid enough to leave the tunnels unguarded, Mr. Majors?"

Harley shrugged as the man started walking toward him. "Didn't really give it much thought, actually. Burns ain't the brightest bulb in the box, from what I've seen." To the side he caught a glimpse of one of the flashlights they kept at each tunnel entrance. Big, heavy and metal, that would do the job. If he could reach it.

The man advanced, his arms dropping to swing at his sides. He reminded Harley of a cheesy B-movie soldier, fresh off the mold. "I'll have to ask you to return to your room, Mr. Majors. I'm afraid the ranch is on lock-down at the moment."

Harley edged closer to the flashlight, careful to move only a few inches at a time. "It's my ranch. I say whether it's on lock-down or not."

He lunged just as the guard reached for him, the other man's fingertips just grazing his arm. Grabbing the flashlight he waited until the guard was nearly on top of him. He swung the light in a wide arch, catching the man on the back of the head with a resounding thunk. The guard slumped over him, and Harley pushed him off then ran down the tunnel, flashlight in one hand, phone in the other.

Not bothering to use the light, he felt his way to the spot where he and Monica had escaped his bedroom. Ducking through the portal, he went to the closet and put clothes on, wincing at the bite of material over his wound. Then he grabbed a rifle and a handgun off the top shelf, loaded both, stuffed the gun in his waistband and headed back into the tunnels with the rifle slung over one arm.

Using the flashlight this time, he traveled deep into the lesser known passages at the back of the compound. It felt like forever, but finally he emerged from the cellar at the dude ranch, relieved that Burns seemed to have forgotten about this offshoot of the main compound. He hurried across to the bunkhouse and peeked in the corner of the window. The clock on the wall read four-thirty in the morning, and six cowboys were just starting to rise from their bunks. They'd probably enjoy a change of pace today, he thought as he knocked on the door before letting himself in.

The men greeted him with silent nods. Devon, the dude ranch foreman held out a hand. "You're up early, boss." He examined Harley's face closely before adding, "And not lookin' so hot, if you don't mind my sayin' so. What can we do for you?"

Shaking the man's hand, Harley let the rifle slip

down his arm and propped it against the wall. "As a matter of fact, there is. I don't suppose the strange guys acting like they own the place on the main compound have been up here to see you?"

A couple of the guys in back snickered. "Well, two of 'em came out the other day. Decided they weren't quite ready for country life though, and skedaddled back to your side of the property pretty quick when Barney looked sideways at 'em."

Harley grinned. Barney, a two-thousand pound bull kept for on site rodeos and the occasional breeding tended to have that effect on people, even though he was quite gentle. For a bull.

"Glad to hear it," he said, wincing as he leaned against the door, pain shooting up through his side. "I don't know if you heard out here, but I married the daughter of the man in charge of those guys." He figured they could clarify details later. Right now there were more important things to worry about. "Burns, the leader, wasn't real happy that I married Monica, and now he's got control of the ranch, and was holding me hostage until just a few hours ago. Thought you guys might be able to give me a hand in running him off my property."

Nods and murmurs of approval met his request, and Devon settled a short Australian-style felt hat on his head. "Just tell us what you need, boss. We'll have those guys out of here in no time."

* * *

Two hours later, Harley peered out from his position in the park facing the clinic. Two of the cowboys had gone to secure the main building, and two more had raided the rooms Burns' had in the hotel, tying up four people before rejoining Devon and Harley. Now the four of them had surrounded the clinic, and Harley had begrudgingly let Devon lead the other men inside while he waited here, behind a tall lilac bush to pick off anyone who managed to slip away. It was killing him not being there to personally capture Burns, but his side had started bleeding again and Devon had pointed out that if Harley hesitated even for a second, Burns would kill him.

So he waited, gritting his teeth as he listened to shouts and yells rise up inside the building, punctuated with the pop of several guns. Finally Burns' men stumbled out, hands held high as Devon and his men steered them to the park at gunpoint. Harley squinted into the sun, his brows drawing together as he took stock of the three prisoners and Ben, who didn't look any worse for the wear, thank god.

"Where's Burns?" he asked as the cowboys tied up the interlopers and settled in to figure out what to do with them. Harley had called the FBI in Vegas from the dude ranch, but they hadn't heard anything from Monica, and the woman on the other end had sounded skeptical. Hopefully someone would show up soon. If not, they'd have to figure out how to deal with Burns and his men. Maybe the Mexican government would take him off their hands, if the US government wouldn't.

"You didn't see him?" Devon turned to glance back at the buildings. "Someone slipped out the back just as we were going in. Tanner went after him, but saw him head around front and thought you'd get him." He shook his head and finished tying off a knot across one of the bodyguards' wrists. "Give me a minute and I'll go after him."

"Thanks, but I've got this one." Harley slung the rifle back over his shoulder. "Just stay with these guys until we can figure out what to do next, okay? I'll get Burns."

Chapter Eighteen

"We're almost at the turnoff. Is there anything else you can tell us that might help, Ms. Burns?"

"It's Mrs. Majors. And not that I can think of," Monica said, holding on to the handle above the car door as they sped toward the ranch. FBI Agent Kelsey Monroe had shown up at the office at six that morning, and when Monica told her the whole story, she hadn't hesitated to round up a team. Apparently Daniels, the undercover agent, was supposed to check in a week ago and they'd lost track of Burns when he went silent. Agent Monroe had sent someone out to check the cab companies for the recordings, and had tried to send Monica to the hospital. Frantic to get back to the ranch, Monica had refused and after a quick patch job on her shoulder, she'd joined Monroe's team. All she could think of during the endless drive back was getting back to Harley in time. If Burns had hurt him...

"We're treating this like a raid," Monroe said as she

took the turn-off and pulled into the empty parking
lot. She looked over her sunglasses at Monica with a
stern expression. "You are not to leave this vehicle
under any circumstances. You'll get in the way, and
there's a good chance you could be shot or taken
hostage. I need to know you're not going to add to
the problem. Understood?"

Monica nodded agreeably. She had no intention of
waiting even though what Monroe said made sense.
She had to find Harley. That was the only thing that
mattered, now that she was sure Burns would be
taken into custody.

Monroe stared at her for a long moment, then
shook her head and got out of the car. The two
agents in the back got out, and five more exited the
second SUV that had followed them down. Monica
watched as they fanned out, several going around the
fence on each side, and Monroe leading the others
through the front gate. She waited, expecting some
sort of commotion, but the minutes ticked by and it
never came. Five minutes later, she opened the door
and jogged to the main building, peering carefully
around the corner into the compound.

The gravel roads were deserted. Where was everyone? She eased around to the front of the building
then sprinted across to the alley between the center
rows of buildings. Moving slowly, she crept toward
the back of the compound, stopping at every concrete
corner and getting more worried by the second. Why

wasn't there any noise?

Finally she reached the end, and stood with her back to Aphrodite's, looking sideways at the back of the compound. Across the road stood the chapel, and a group seemed to be gathered in the park to the right. The bright white letters on the FBI vests stood out in stark relief, but where had the horses come from? And were those real live cowboys?

As she watched, agents began leading handcuffed men toward the front gate. A sigh of relief escaped her lips, and when the last agent went past, she jogged out into the road, hoping Harley would be with the remaining people mingling in the park. She almost didn't see him half-hidden in the shadows at the front of the chapel, except the sun glinted off metal as she reached the center of the road. Stopping mid-stride, she almost called to him before noting the raised gun, and the absolute focus in his posture. He was aiming at some point behind her, and she instinctively turned to look.

A low whooshing sound was the only warning she got before she was knocked backwards to the ground. Dazed, she heard the pop of guns a long ways off as she tried to sit up, but couldn't quite manage. Her arms felt so heavy, and a dull burning pain set in just above her knee as a shadow fell across her face.

"Monica? Oh god...someone get Ben!" Strong arms lifted her, cradling her against a warm, familiar chest.

She forced the words from her mind onto her lips,

wondering why it was so hard to speak. "Harley, I--"

"Shh...don't talk. The clinic is close, and Ben will fix you up good as new. I promise."

Monica closed her eyes, whimpering softly as she was laid on a soft surface and that warm, comforting feeling left. She started shivering, unable to keep her teeth from clattering together. Cold. She was so cold...

* * *

Monica woke slowly to the sound of someone snoring next to her. The green brocade canopy above her was dimly lit with light coming in through the narrow windows near the ceiling and she grinned, recognizing Harley's bed. Turning her head, she saw him sprawled out on his stomach beside her and she couldn't resist the urge to touch him. He stirred as she ran her fingers over his warm, bare skin and she marveled at the connection she felt to this rough and tumble man.

"Look who's awake," he said, his voice soft and husky as he turned to smile at her. She tried to roll to her side, but a shooting pain in her leg vetoed the move.

"Ow." She winced, remembering the events of the day before. "Did I get shot?"

Harley nodded, gently stroking the side of her neck with his knuckles. "I've never been so scared in my life. When I saw you go down..." he shook his head, leaning down to press a kiss to her lips. "Thank god the bullet didn't hit anything vital and went all the way through. I had Ben clean out the wound and bandage you up and then we brought you here. I thought you'd be more comfortable at home than at the clinic."

She nodded, her heart swelling at how good the word *home* sounded. "Thank you. I'll have to thank the doctor too. Did you see who shot me? Did you get him?"

Propping himself up on one elbow, Harley looked down at her, his expression unreadable. "I got him. I'm sorry, honey, but it was Burns. He warned me he was going to make it so you couldn't run away again. When he shot you..."

"It's okay." Monica closed her eyes, trying to sort through the conflicting feelings swirling in her head. Guilt warred with pain and abandonment, but it had been so long since Burns had been anything but someone to be avoided that the feelings were muted. She mainly felt numb.

Harley pulled her into his arms, cradling her head against his broad chest. She melted against him, soaking up his warmth and listening to his heart beat steady under her ear. He stroked her arm and kissed the top of her head.

"I told you not to come back. Why didn't you run like I told you to?" he asked. "You could have been killed showing up here."

She pulled out of his embrace so she could look at him. "I told you I'd be back. I'm through running, Harley. I'm also done taking orders from men - or anyone, for that matter. From now on I do what I want, when I want, understood?"

He grinned, amusement sparkling in his eyes. "Yes, ma'am. Does that mean I'm taking orders from you now?"

She looked up thoughtfully, pretending to give the matter serious thought. "Yes, I believe it does." She grinned. "Tell me you love me."

"I love you more than life itself," he replied, leaning forward for a kiss. "Do I get a reward for good behavior?" he murmured against her lips. She kissed him back, meeting his tongue with her own as he devoured her mouth. When she finally pulled back, her whole body was simmering with desire and happiness. Finally she belonged.

"Oh yeah," she breathed, smoothing her hand down the center of his chest. "I think we both deserve a reward." She hooked an arm around his neck and pulled him down over her as she rolled to her back, whispering in his ear as he nibbled at her neck.

"I love you too."

Epilogue

Six months later...

"There you are," Harley said as he tried to catch his breath after climbing up the stone steps to the far back tower of the castle. Monica and some of the other girls from the ranch had turned the room into sort of a bridal war room, and as he stepped inside he was greeted with four pairs of female eyes staring in mock disapproval.

"You know you're not supposed to be up here," Betsy said from her chair at the head of a long, heavy wooden table. "This better be important. Veronica was just telling us about how Cha--"

"Shut up, Betsy." Veronica shook her head. "Never mind, boss. I assume you want your wife for something?"

Monica laughed, extricating herself from a pile of multicolored silky fabrics. "I'll be right back, ladies. I'm sure Harley wouldn't be here if it wasn't important. Look at his face." She winked at him as she made her way across the room, laughing when he wrinkled his nose.

"I'm sure we all know exactly what he's after," Amy chimed in sarcastically. Dressed in a long blue gown that matched the castle, she was the castle entertainment chair, though Harley wasn't sure how much longer she'd last. She didn't seem to be getting along well with the man he'd put in charge of the keep. The other two women laughed as Monica pulled the door shut and leaned in for a kiss.

"Don't mind them dear," she said, her lips warm and inviting as they moved against his. "They're just jealous. Men in leather tend to do that to women."

He grinned, glad he hadn't changed after his shift at the bar. Wrapping his arms around her and ravishing her mouth, he bent her back over his arm in a dramatic gesture. When he finally released her, she swayed against him, her eyes half-closed with pleasure.

"Mmm...gonna take me right here in the hall, tough guy?"

Harley sighed, shaking his head wistfully as he reached for the envelope he'd tucked into his vest. "Sorry, darlin'. I promised I'd deliver this right away."

Monica took it and slid her thumb under the flap. Unfolding the paper within, she read it twice, the second time looking at him like she was in some sort of trance.

"Did you read it?" she asked, folding it again. He shook his head.

"No, but I talked to her. I told her to write the letter. Said you'd let her know if you're interested."

She went to a narrow window and sat on the stone ledge. "I don't understand though. How did she find me? And does she know there's nothing left – that we donated all of Burns' assets to that adoption group?"

"She knows." Harley went to stand beside her, stroking her hair with one hand as she leaned into him. "It's not money she's interested in. She just wants to meet her daughter. She contacted Burns' lawyer when she heard he was dead. Apparently she's been wanting to meet you for a long time."

Monica looked up at him with glassy eyes as the door opened and Betsy came out, a worried look on her face. "Is everything okay?" One look at Monica, and she stomped up to Harley. "What did you do to her?"

"It's not him," Monica said, rising to her feet with a wane smile. She held up the letter. "It's my...mother, I guess. She wants to meet me."

Betsy grinned. "Well that's great news, isn't it? Invite her to the wedding. Then we'll all get to meet her, and you'll have plenty of support if things go sour."

"I couldn't...I mean, that would be weird, don't you think?" Monica wiped her eyes gingerly. "If something happens..."

Betsy flipped a hand up carelessly. "Nothing's going to happen. It will be a great day. Now come on, we've got a ton of things to do before the big day. Only two weeks to go." She grabbed Monica's hand and pulled her back toward the door. "Go away, brother. You can have her back in a few hours."

Harley waited for Monica's nod, then blew her a kiss before she disappeared into the other room. Letting out a sigh, he started back down the stairs again. It was going to be an interesting summer.

About the Author

A full-time webmistress by day, Jamie DeBree writes steamy, action-packed romantic suspense late into the night. Her goal is to create the perfect blend of sensual attraction, emotional tension and fast-paced adventure, similar to the television crime dramas she's hopelessly addicted to.

Born in Billings Montana, she resides there with her husband and two over-sized lap dogs. She reads in a wide variety of genres including romance, erotica, action/adventure, thriller, horror and literary.

For information on upcoming books, visit jamiedebree.com.